BACK CHECK

Boston Rebels, book 2

RJ SCOTT

V.L. LOCEY

Love Lane Books

Copyright

Dedication

To my family who accepts me and all my foibles and quirks. Even the plastic banana in my holster.
VL Locey

Always for my family.
RJ Scott

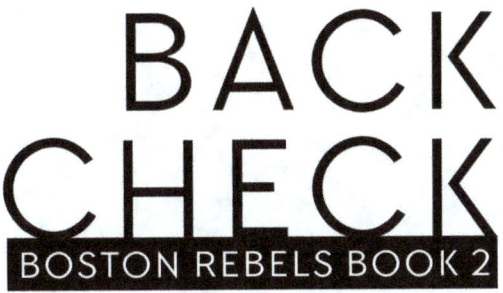

BACK CHECK
BOSTON REBELS BOOK 2

RJ SCOTT &
V.L. LOCEY

Love Lane Books

Chapter One

Isaac

THE BOX ARRIVED ON A TUESDAY.

Coincidentally, the same day I received the worst news in a phone call from the oncologist, and right about the moment I lost the last of my hope that we would ever find a donor to match Sophie.

"The HLA markers came back at six or less in all the potential donors," Dr. Carmichael said in her quiet, supportive tone. "I'm so sorry, Isaac."

"Then we use one of the people that match six? At this point, surely that's all we *can* do?" We needed a donor, but we couldn't find one. Without a donor, Sophie couldn't have the chemo. Without the chemo, she'd die. It was a simple chain of events, but we were stuck on part one.

Sophie fussed in my arms, wriggled, and butted my shoulder as she tried to fight sleep. We'd been up all night, watching kids shows and singing nursery rhymes. My eyes scratched with exhaustion and my throat was sore from a hundred iterations of "Wheels on the Bus."

"I wish it was. Having the best possible match means less risk of Sophie's body rejecting the new stem cells or her new immune cells reacting against her other body cells. It would be disingenuous of me to suggest that taking a chance on a mismatched transplant would be right for Sophie at the present time."

"But we've run out of options. Tell me what else we can do."

"We'll keep searching."

"I read a transplant from a relative whose tissue was a half-match to Sophie. What about me?"

"A haploidentical transplant you mean? I'm sorry, you're not a match for that," she reminded me gently. "And I'm guessing you still haven't tracked down her biological father?"

I'd tried. I went to the bar where my sister had worked, which was staffed by people who lasted a few months and drifted away and were mostly from the University of Tampa Campus, covering peak times of the year. They remembered my sister, recalled that Ashley was vivacious, a little wild, beautiful, funny, but not one of them knew anything below the surface. She hadn't left any kind of footprint at the college or the bar or the hundreds of places in between that could help me track down Sophie's sperm donor. The fact I couldn't control this situation was driving me insane, and the baby daddy situation was yet another thing I'd never gotten out of my sister, and never would, as she'd died the day Sophie was born.

Despite becoming an uncle, then a single parent, in one

terrifying twenty-four-hour period, I got through it and came out the other side, grieving, but wholly focused on Sophie and what she needed. I didn't even think twice about putting everything on hold for the tiny scrap of a thing who searched for her momma, but was left with me. That had been two years ago. Sophie had just passed her second birthday, and I had the photos to prove that she was a physical presence in my life—a beautiful smiling angel with dark hazel eyes and fine blonde hair that was nothing like her mom's or mine. I couldn't bear to think that these might be the last photos I'd ever have of her with a cake.

We'd tried everything, every database, every resource, and I knew Doc Carmichael was the best oncologist for Sophie. Every cent I had went to Sophie's care, but I felt helpless because I couldn't do anything. I was out of money and losing hope. I wished I could heal her just with the force of my love, but miracles like that didn't happen.

Sophie murmured against my neck. She was running a temperature, but not a normal one from teething or a mild fever that new parents expect. This was from a poison inside my daughter's blood, and it was slowly gripping her and pulling her away from me, minute by agonizing minute. Some days, when I looked into her eyes, I saw nothing but a bright future for her, with all the possibilities of what she could be someday, there for her to take. Then the shadows would fall in my own eyes and all I could see was pain and loss. Now, I don't know if I can live without her. I'd lost everyone close to me—my parents to Hurricane Wilma, my grandparents who'd faded from old age, and then Ashley herself.

It was just Sophie and me now.

And I was losing her too.

"I wouldn't even know how to narrow it down," I said in defeat. "Aside from erecting a sign on every corner and asking if some random guy knew my sister, I have no way of knowing anything at all."

Dr. Carmichael made a noise that sounded as if she was sucking her teeth. She never once mentioned that my sister's wild days had left us backed into a corner—she was nothing but supportive—but even I wanted to bury my face in my hands and scream at Ashley's life choices. If we knew the sperm donor then we'd be able to move onto an alternative solution, but we didn't, and Sophie was dying.

"As for good news, her last results were encouraging…"

I didn't even listen. I'd heard the hope in her voice before about good results that implied Sophie would make it through this, when I knew in black and white terms that she wouldn't.

Neither would I.

"… so, I'll see you for your appointment on Friday and stay strong, Isaac. Give Sophie a kiss for me."

She wrapped up the conversation, with the kiss line, and I wondered if it was something that all pediatric oncologists learned in college. *Send them a kiss, connect the parent to the child after delivering bad news, always sound positive.*

"I will, thank you, doctor."

The call ended at the same moment the doorbell rang, leaving me no time to dwell in the isolation of my hallway when someone needed me. Albeit the postman, who was probably dropping off a parcel meant for one of my neighbors, which happened often, as I was the only one in the vicinity who worked from home.

"One for you, Mr. Miller," the postal worker announced with a grin and handed me a battered box wound with enough tape to start a shop. He scanned the parcel and asked me to sign, then I shut the door and rattled the box to work out what someone had sent. It certainly wasn't a professional wrapping job, so I didn't imagine it was merch from any of my clients.

I carried it and Sophie through to the kitchen. Sophie was now sleeping on my shoulder, her tiny hands twisted in my shirt, and thankfully, she seemed cooler than earlier. I placed her into the rocker, which was locked into a permanent position in the breakfast nook, then gave the parcel another shake.

Graphic designer killed in exploding parcel incident.

Sophie murmured in her sleep, her eyes opening briefly, as she searched the room for me.

"Dadda," she whined, arching against the belt that held her secure, and then fisted her hands when I didn't lift her out fast enough. I'd gone to her immediately, all thoughts of parcels and bombs and life just gone in that instant she needed me. I bet any nanny worth their salt would tell me I shouldn't carry her with me, but this was Sophie and my time with her might be limited. I wanted every snuggle and moment of love I could get. She pushed one hand into my hair and stared at me with an expression that meant this could go one of two ways. She could start to cry because she was exhausted, in pain, or just generally crabby, or she could melt in my arms and cling to me.

"Hey, baby girl," I whispered against her neck. She

smelled so good, and she loved me and needed me so much. The grief welled up from me so fast it took my breath away.

"Dadda," she murmured again and then closed her eyes and snuggled in for more love. My heart filled with love, but the sorrow in my chest grew stronger daily, and it was making it harder to keep it there. I'd worked my way through the steps of grief. Hell, denial had lasted an hour before I was on the internet googling everything from cutting-edge drugs to mystical solutions. I would do anything for Sophie, but I felt hopeless and lost because I couldn't be the dad she needed right now.

One-handed, I attempted to open the box, hacking through the tape in a messy uncoordinated way until the top was shredded and I was finally able to pin back the tabs. There was an envelope at the top, and opening that was an exercise in frustration, but at last I was able to pull out the note. It was short and to the point, and from a name I recognized. Jillian McAfee, an old roommate of Ashley's at UT—who majored in chemistry or something equally intelligent and had been as quiet as Ashley was vivacious. Last I saw her was just after Sophie was diagnosed when I'd been looking for clues as to the identity of Sophie's baby daddy. Jillian summed up Ashley as someone who flitted from person to person and didn't have a steady partner, adding that Ashley was confident and sassy and always smiling. Still, she couldn't give me a clue as to the identity of the sperm donor.

"This is from a lady who knew your momma," I told a sleeping Sophie.

Hi, you might not remember me, but I roomed with Ashley for a while. These are some of her things that I'd mixed in with mine when she didn't come back for the final semester. Hope all's good with you. Love Jillian.

As notes went it wasn't earthshattering, but I was excited to see some of Ashley's things that I could put away for when Sophie was older. *If there was a later.* I rubbed at the abrupt pain in my chest, forced away the sorrow, and focused on the positives. We *would* find a way to get a match. Somehow.

At the top were a couple of sparkly leotards, seeing them brought back so many memories of Ashley dressing up in things like this and giving our grandparents impromptu dance recitals. They hadn't happened much after we lost them, seemed as if nothing nice happened after that, but hell, I wasn't going to think about that right now.

"Come on, Soph, let's take this into the garden room." I carried coffee out there first, then returned for the box. Sophie never woke for one second. When I finally got to sit in the comfy chair that was my happy place, Sophie tucked into my neck, I pulled the box onto the small side table and picked out the next item. It was a calculator, an old Casio, that I couldn't believe for one second my sister had ever used. Neither of us were gifted with mathematical brains, she a dancer and me an artist, but on the back, scratched into the plastic, was her name. I missed her so much, for all that happened when we were growing up, for all the obstacles in our way, for her leaving too soon. I missed her like a limb.

A stuffed toy followed next, a giraffe wearing an orange T-shirt, and attached to the T-shirt was a key ring from the bar she worked at—Branson's Beach Pub. There were some postcards of London, a place she always wanted to visit, and a photo of Mom, Dad, me, and her from way back when we were just youngsters without a care in the world. We looked so innocent, me ten and her eight, the year before a tropical storm became something more, and Hurricane Wilma took Mom and Dad without stopping.

There was something else wedged in at the bottom, a textbook or something, but when I levered it out, I realized it was stuck because it had a lock on it, like one of those old-fashioned secret diaries, although there was no sign of the key. I stared at it for the longest time, torn between opening it and then struck by the fact there might be a name in there that would help find a connection to Sophie. Was it an actual journal? I went to fetch a knife then thought better of carrying Sophie at the same time and placed her back in her chair. *Just give me a few moments, sweet girl.*

I had the lock broken in no more than two twists of the knife, then placed it carefully on the counter. Sophie seemed content to sleep where she was, and with a prayer to the goddesses of luck and hope, I opened the journal to page one.

It *was* a diary of sorts, dated, but there were random notes scattered in the margins, a reminder for a haircut, a shift list for the bar, a list of possible nail polish colors, and a lecture schedule that was pasted on page five. A bobby pin marked that page, and it was oddly bright with a smiling ladybird against the subtle cream paper. My hope shifted to despair when I didn't immediately find the words baby daddy with an equal sign and then a name.

But when I got further in, the posts were more of a diary. There were entries for deadlines for work, even a note about a three-hundred-dollar tip and what she was going to spend it on.

Then I saw the first note of interest, dated Christmas Eve 2017. I hadn't seen her at all that Christmas, or even much at all the entire year. She'd been at college, getting on with her life. We had at least exchanged texts, but they never went much past the "are you okay, yes I am," kind of exchange. Too many wasted days.

"Met HG tonight, dark eyes, muscles, sexy man, swoon."

Well, that didn't narrow the pool, but it was the only mention so far of this nebulous *man* and the initials HG. That could be Harry, Henry, *anything*.

I went through the next few entries. HG appeared a couple of times, and she seemed interested in him.

Was HG Sophie's father? The timing was right. Christmas 2017. There were smaller notes, a clipping of a red low-cut dress, and then there in black and white was the first clue I had.

29th HG puck drop 7. Will call ticket. Reminder NYE 8-3, nails = scarlet lake.

I flicked back to her schedule, and yep, she was working New Year's 2017 from eight p.m. to three on New Year's Day, so that was one detail I could rule out. Puck drop, I guess that is hockey? I'm not the world's best expert at hockey, or sports in general, but the one thing I did know is that pucks were found in hockey. Was she meeting someone at the hockey game? Was HG a hockey fan? That narrowed it down a bit. Maybe I needed to reach out to the local NHL team or to one of the smaller teams? I didn't know enough, but I had initials and that was a start. Then I saw the words Hockey Guy, and my heart sank. HG was just short for Hockey Guy? Had she even known the man's name? How could she conceive a baby and not know the sperm donor's name? A flush of anger vanished as soon as I glanced at Sophie because no connection that made her could be wrong.

I scanned the rest of the journal, broken up once by Sophie waking up grumpy and hungry, but by the time midnight rolled around I knew without a doubt that Ashley had met and hooked up with a hockey fan she called Hockey Guy, or HG for short, because it was the only thing that made sense.

Which is why for the opening game of the preseason, against Tampa, I left Sophie with June, a neighbour and retired nurse, who had babysat for me in the past. Dressed head to toe in neon orange, I headed to the Tampa Arena with three huge signs I'd drawn, determined to get the attention of every single hockey fan as they went into the place.

Sophie needed help so there I stood half-naked with face paint, looking like a carrot. I couldn't get a ticket to the game, but if queuing fans read the signs and went to get themselves tested with the hospital to see if they were a match to Sophie, then it was a win. Maybe, somewhere, within the twenty-thousand people at the arena, HG might be there, and I *was* going to find him.

Because it really was Sophie's last chance.

And I refused to let someone else die on my watch.

Chapter Two

Joachim

"THE CEILING IS YELLOW," I POINTED OUT FOR THE FOURTH time.

That little aspect of the home I was looking at didn't seem to bother the realtor as much as it did me. Who would paint a tidy little home right across the street from Wigwam Pond in such atrocious colors? The pond had been a big selling point and had drawn me to the listing. I liked being by water of any kind, the sea preferably, but the prices for homes on the waterfront had made my eyeballs pop. Of course, my condo on the beach down in Florida had been crazy expensive, but it had been part of a lifestyle that was not my reality anymore. Extravagance led to excess, which led to abusing booze, which led to… well, looking at a home in a small Boston suburb that had a sunflower-yellow ceiling.

"Nothing that some paint can't cover up," Madeline, the chipper Realtor—was there any other kind?—brightly announced, then led me from the living room to the kitchen where, thank God, the ceiling was white. "This room was recently redone and has all new modern appliances. Mrs. Lafgrain will love cooking you those big meals when you come home from your hockey games all sweaty and revved up."

"Löfgren," I politely corrected the tiny blond with the appreciative gaze. "Like a loaf of bread and a smile. Loaf. Grin. And there is no missus."

Her pale eyes lit up. "Oh, well what a shame." She sidled closer, pushing me back into a corner as if she was on a mission to back check me. She was way worse than an offensive rush heading for the net.

I smiled down at her, then asked to see the rest of the three bedroom, two bath home. It was a rather nice place. Built in the fifties, it still had some of the charm of the era, even with the upgrades. Shame they'd not seen the need to upgrade that damn yellow ceiling. The tour lasted about forty minutes, and by the time it was over, Madeline was hanging off every word I said, as well as simply hanging off *me*. Women tended to like to look at me. As did men. I liked looking at both. It was when they got past my looks and discovered what a wreck I was that they tended to shuffle off without a word. Not that I blamed them. I came with steamers full of baggage.

As Madeline held onto my arm and flirted, I circled the home a final time, checking out the chain link fencing. Maybe I could get a dog now. New team, new town, new home, new life. Might as well add a new dog to the mix.

"So, what do we think?" Madeline asked, leaning in to make sure that I noticed that she had unbuttoned the top button of her prim white blouse. She had the hint of lovely breasts, but I just wasn't interested in hooking up with anyone. I'd learned a lot in my most recent stint in rehab, prime being that Joachim had to fix Joachim before Joachim could be with another person. And I was trying my best to glue the bits of myself back together. It was a lonely task, but I was used to loneliness.

"I think that if they're willing to come down in price, I'll take it." I named a figure I'd be willing to pay and she pouted, her freshly touched-up red lips puckering.

"Hmmm."

"It will cost me three thousand to get the living room ceiling presentable."

She nodded, then leaned in to press those lovely breasts more tightly into my arm. In the past, I'd have rolled this eager blond right in the kids' beds in that charming little home and not thought twice about it. Probably, we'd have had a few bottles of wine from that new fridge in the kitchen first. There was usually always booze first. And second. And third. Sex went with addiction and fame. Not that I was famous here, but down in the Sunshine State, everyone knew my name. Mostly from my time playing hockey, but many from the "incidents" that occurred during that time.

"Let me give them a call and see what they say." She winked. I smiled down at her with all my charm, which was considerable according to my past lovers. I'd bedded numerous people in my thirty-three years. Yes, I had a pleasing face and a nice body. It was what was inside my skull that was a gin-soaked work in progress.

"You do that. I'll cross the street to look at the pond

again." I patted her hand, then peeled her fingers away from my sleeve. I'd had to pull on a sweater this morning because the temperature on my patio had been below sixty. I shuddered to think of what it'd be like here in winter. I hated the snow and cold, which was why I had been thrilled to play in Florida for so long. Crossing the road, I entered the park area, the smell of pond water rich on the dry air. Not wanting to make the realtor search for me, I stayed within view of my new home and watched a man fishing from the shore. Now *that* I could enjoy. I'd loved taking deep-sea fishing trips with my old teammates over the summer. I never went back to Switzerland when the season was over. There was nothing there for me. My parents had both died within the past ten years, first my mother and then my father. I had no siblings and only one cousin, Elias, who still lived in Zermatt. His disgust with my addiction and bisexuality had ended any warm feelings that might've been there from childhood. Family was a thing I'd always yearned for but had slowly been stripped away from me.

And why is that, Joachim?

Well, Dr. Jane, probably because I drink to excess, then make poor choices.

Very good, Joachim. We must own our addictions before we can move past them.

"Oh, here you are!" I looked over my shoulder to see Madeline scurrying to me, her boobs close to bouncing out of her push-up bra. "They said they'd take your offer. You *did* say it was cash, correct?"

"That's correct." Everything that I'd owned in Tampa Bay, right down to my Porsche, had been liquidated when

I'd been sold to Boston—who had to have been insane to offer me a cool million a year when all I was worth was a bag of soggy jockstraps, according to the press in Florida. Sadly, they weren't far off. But I was sober and had something to prove to the NHL and myself. This little house with the fenced-in yard just a short train ride from the barn felt like a good place to rebuild my life. Again.

"Well let's go back to my office and—" Her cell chirruped. "Well damn, it's my husband." She gave me a guilty look that made me smile to myself. "He'll meet us at my office. He's a Rebels fan and wants to meet you."

I sniggered inside, then led the lovely lady back to her car. My rental sat in the driveway behind her blue Cadillac. I gave the little house a fond look, then slid behind the wheel of my Buick. My new life started here, and this time, I would *not* fuck it up. A man only got so many second chances.

IT FELT ODD TO BE SITTING IN A COFFEE SHOP SURROUNDED by my new teammates after just two days on the team. The team had their own back room, and we pulled two brightly painted tables together upon our arrival. Now we were sipping lattes and frappés while we were shoving baked goods into our faces and talking about the upcoming season. Down in Tampa, the team had met up in a bar after practices. Oh, the good times I'd had. I'd start the day off with a mimosa or a simple screwdriver—it was orange juice so that counted as breakfast—and things would go downhill from there. Bean Town Brews seemed a much safer choice for a man who was still looking for a nearby AA meeting to attend.

"Oh! So, I ran into this really cool artist who said they could do renditions of our D&D characters for us!" Austin Rowe, the cousin of Tennant, Brady, and Jamie, whom I'd played with down in the Bay, announced. "Well, I didn't run into her, I kind of commissioned her online. But she's local and really good!"

"When did we say we were doing D&D?" Moral asked while ripping off the top of his fourth apple crumb muffin. He was a big, boisterous redhead from Montreal and incredibly likable. I glanced from Moral to Marquis, who was stirring a cup of tea while reading a book on his phone. He glanced up at the mention of role-playing, his dark eyes narrowing as he assessed us all over the top of his stylish eyeglasses.

"When did we agree to this? Was it when I was overseas during the summer?" Marquis asked, the winger's spoon stalling in his tea.

"Austin said we talked about it," Renco, the Rebels goalie, chimed in as he looked from me to the windows at the front of the coffee shop.

We all stared at Austin, who blushed red as a beet. He was a cute kid, filled with fire and that talent all the damn Rowes seemed to possess. I felt so out of place, and yet, oddly welcomed by this small group of men. Many, it seemed, were either allies or out, like Xander and Austin. That made the locker room a much more accepting and pleasant place to be for a bi newcomer.

"We'd talked about it that night in the bar in Aruba," Austin stated, then smiled at his boyfriend, a barista, who winked back as he passed our table holding a tray filled with coffee and treats.

"How drunk were we all?" Marquis enquired as he resumed stirring his tea.

"Uhm, not super," Austin answered, his gaze on his boyfriend as he spoke. Young love. How endearing. Perhaps someday I'd find someone to gaze at with open adoration like Austin did his Robbie. "I was sober."

"I think I remember a conversation about a druid," Moral said around his mouthful of muffin. Austin snapped back from admiring his boyfriend's backside.

"Yes! See! You said you'd be a druid, Moral. And Marquis wanted to be a wizard of some sort and Xander said he wanted to be a dwarf with a big ax."

"Is that a euphemism?" Marquis tossed out. We all chuckled.

"Renco is going to be a bard, and I'm going to be a monk," Austin said with a grin.

"Not sure that fits you right now," Moral teased, making Austin blush yet again.

"What are you going to be, Joachim?" Rowe enquired. My cherry tart stalled halfway to my mouth. My new teammates all stared at me openly.

"Oh, well... I, uhm, I've never played that game before. I'm not sure if I'll have time with a new house and all the team systems I have to learn and—"

"You've got time. We'll play on the plane and shit. You know what you'd be good as?" Moral pointed at me with half of a muffin, crumbs falling to the table from his baked good and his beard. "A paladin. That's a holy warrior who is bound to an oath. You've got this new sobriety that you've sworn to, and you fight like a motherfucking warrior!"

I nodded. It was common knowledge that I'd spent the summer in rehab drying out. I wasn't ashamed of my faults. We all had them. "Okay well, sure, I can see that the comparison fits, but the point still stands that I've never played this game before."

"It's really simple," Austin said then scratched the soft little whiskers on his chin. "Well, not so much simple, but complicated in a simple way. We'll walk you through it. Robbie is going to be an owl-bear!"

"Oh that's… interesting." I gave everyone a smile. I could make the effort because I really needed something to focus on right now. "Sure, I guess I'd love to be a…"

"Paladin," Austin reminded me.

"Yeah. A paladin."

Austin fist bumped me. "Yes! This will be awesome. These kinds of things are great for building team spirit. Tennant and the Railers play Pokémon, so I didn't want to do that. This is awesome! Robbie and I will print out character creation forms!"

Austin left his seat to go chat with his boyfriend at the counter. That was when Xander arrived looking freshly scrubbed and tense. He flopped down beside Renco, then gave us all a nod.

"Sorry I'm late. I had to meet with Sinclair and the other coaches." Everyone else looked at him expectantly and I wondered what I was missing.

"And?" Moral prompted.

Xander seemed shellshocked. "They're definitely putting captain to a team vote and want me to put myself out there." Moral clapped him on the back, Marquis and Renco congratulated him. "I haven't been this nervous since I asked Tiffany Lankowski to the junior prom."

"We're voting for captain?" I couldn't help sounding surprised—I'd never heard that happen before.

"Yep," Moral stated, then dunked a muffin top into his coffee. "I'm going to vote for Xander."

"You're the natural choice now that Brady has retired," Marquis said.

I didn't know the team well enough to plant my flag, but the Rebels had strong leadership and I knew Xander. He was a strong voice in the room, and I respected him on the ice.

Austin re-joined us with his phone out and his eyes shiny and wet.

"Hey, guys, did you see this story coming out of Tampa?"

Everyone looked at me.

"I didn't do it," I quickly said as I lifted my hands up in innocence. "I was here in Boston."

"No, it's nothing bad like you're used to," Austin blurted out. Xander swatted him upside the head. The boy's eyes bugged out, and his soft cheeks turned scarlet. "Oh! No, I didn't mean you did bad stuff! Being drunk isn't bad. Well, it's bad when you run off the road and hit a mailbox. It's not bad in a bad way. It's, uhm… well, it's just an addiction right, and you're not drinking anymore so it's all okay. No, well, okay in that you've stopped drinking and are now—"

"It's okay, Rowe, I know what you meant, and it's fine.

I did some pretty fucked up things when I was abusing alcohol."

Austin wilted a bit. "Okay, thanks. I didn't mean to imply that addictions are bad. I mean they are! No, not bad like bad but—"

"It's okay, kid. Just move onto the news story." I chuckled. Moral lobbed a chunk of apple at Austin. He ducked it and the glob smacked Renco in the cheek.

"Right, yeah, so there's this guy down in Florida who's looking for a bone marrow donor for his daughter. He showed up at a preseason hockey game to search for some mysterious fan called 'Hockey Guy,' who the dead mother named as the possible father."

"Shit, so the guy is raising his daughter alone?" Moral asked, the sad news slowing his inhalation of muffins for a moment. "Wait…" He placed his muffin on its plate. "If he's the father, then why is he looking for the father?"

"He's the baby's uncle but has been raising her as her father. It's all super sad and everyone in the league is signing up to see if they're a match for the little girl with leukemia. Look at her." He showed us all an image of an adorable little girl of perhaps two or three and her uncle who was also cute as hell. "We should sign up."

"Of course, we will," Xander stated as if he spoke for us all. Which as the "about to be voted on team captain," he did. On the ice. Not off. But I had no qualms about signing up to see if the tyke could use my bone marrow on some off chance. I'd spent a goodly portion of my life in Florida and had met, and loved, some wonderful people. Hell, who knows, I could have even met the baby's mother somewhere along the line. I had not met the daddy/uncle. He'd have stood out in my mind, a face that was perfectly made and eyes that sad. Yeah, him, I'd have remembered for sure. "Count me in."

The talk turned to sick babies and twenty-sided dice. Life here in Boston was certainly going to be vastly different than it had been down south, but it felt like a good different. I prayed it would be.

Chapter Three

Isaac

"WE HAVE A MATCH," DR. CARMICHAEL SAID BEFORE I'D even sat down. When her office had called this morning and asked me to attend a meeting, I imagined it was more of the same. The work I'd done to spread awareness in Tampa hadn't come to anything yet, and I had nothing but black thoughts. I had to sell the house, but that was a small price to keep searching for a match. If I lost Sophie nothing mattered anyway, so why would I even need a home anymore? The money raised would help toward searching for the miracle. I'd left Sophie with June again, promised I wouldn't be long, and headed for the clinic with the weight of everything sitting heavy on my chest.

"A what?" I gripped the back of the chair. I couldn't have heard right.

"A match. Isaac, you need to sit down."

I couldn't move, let alone sit. In the end, she came over and unpeeled my fingers, and helped me to sit before encouraging me to bend my head. Why was she... *shit...* my head buzzed, and my vision blurred. I gasped for air as my chest tightened like a vise around my heart. *A match. A donor.* My breathing stopped, and I clawed at my shirt to get some air, then a few words filtered through.

"... hockey player, not a fan, although..."

Breathe. Breathe. Breathe.

"... Boston, so if that's okay..."

I listened to her words, holding tight to Dr. Carmichael, when finally, my breathing evened out, but the adrenaline rush was impossible. I was so shaky I couldn't even talk, so she did all the talking for me. It seemed that since my standing outside the hockey arena went viral so quick, it led to a massive bone marrow testing push and several matches were found for other cases as well. She also said I should feel proud for what I'd accomplished.

What about Sophie?

"We have enough of a match to perform a transplant." She sat back down on her chair behind the desk.

"Enough? What do you mean enough? Is this a match or not?" I sounded pissed, but I didn't mean to. Words were impossible to form, and my head was tight with pain.

She held up a hand. "Typically, a donor transplant relationship remains anonymous, but the match threw up something you need to consider."

"What? Is it not a proper match? Should we wait? Do we have time to wait?"

"No, it's something else." She paused a moment. "The match is with Sophie's genetic father."

"We found her dad?" Hope flared inside me. That was the best match surely. There was a chance. Dr. Carmichael talked on and on about confidentiality, contracts, and the team jet, and how it would be beneficial to go elsewhere for treatment, but it was a blur.

"Do I still get to make decisions for her?" I interrupted the spiel, having the vague idea that her father would have more say in her care than I did, and abruptly I was terrified. "Will he do it? Will he save her?" I wasn't listening to a thing she said. "Did he say no?"

She came out from behind her desk, then pulled a chair over next to me and held my hand as I stared into her kind gaze.

"You need to listen to me now," she said, but she was smiling.

"Okay. Tell me he'll do it. Tell me he wants to help."

"Let's start from the beginning."

A CAR PARKED OUTSIDE MY TINY HOUSE, A TOWN CAR, with tinted windows and a driver.

"This is it, Soph," I murmured, and she pressed her cheek to mine. The last twenty-four hours had been a frenzy of activity, and with bags packed and June promising to look after my place, I was heading to Boston and the hockey player who was Sophie's dad. They hadn't given me his name, and I wasn't supposed to tell anyone anything. I couldn't even tell June, and she was the closest thing I had to a friend since taking Sophie into my life. I'd packed everything in three suitcases. Sophie's favorite toys, my laptop so I could try to keep working because God knows who was paying for all of this, and enough clothes for a month. Dr. Carmichael explained the process, but most of it was a blur.

The knock on the door was loud, and I should've opened it already, but that flimsy barrier between me and whoever had sent the car was all that was keeping my panic at bay. I needed a moment to think, to breathe, and I buried my face in Sophie's soft curls, inhaling the scent of her and counting back from ten. Finally, I opened the door. A man in a chauffeur uniform was right there, and he smiled.

"Mr. Bailey?"

I held out a hand. "Isaac." Was it right to shake hands with a chauffeur? Were there rules? *Calm down.*

"Alec." The guy smiled. "Let's get your bags in the car."

I couldn't move, didn't have control over my legs, but Alec picked up two of the bags, put them in the trunk, and returned for the last one before I realized I should be moving. I followed Alec to the car, booster seat in one hand, along with a changing bag containing all her meds and anything else that was vitally important, and Sophie in my other arm. Alec took the seat and expertly fitted it, but I double-checked because I was Sophie's protector, and I wasn't going to let anything hurt her.

"There's water and snacks in here." Alec pressed a button and a door slid open to reveal a compartment that was half refrigerated and half not, complete with chips, fruit, packed sandwiches, and bottles of water. Sophie wriggled in the seat, her eyes alighting on her favorite thing, chips. I pulled out the small bag and gave her some, worrying about all the stupid things, such as whether Alec would be happy with crumbs on the leather seats and how long it would be before Sophie got bored. I had my iPad and phone, saw the charging points, and knew I had everything I needed to keep a wearied toddler entertained, however long this drive was.

Only it wasn't a long journey at all. We headed west to the coast and Naples' private airport, driving past security gates and parking alongside a flashy jet, the kind I've seen in movies where insanely rich people spent stupid money on unrealistic things. The scents of the ocean and a warm breeze flowed over me, and for a few moments, I felt centered. I may have a small place, but living on the Florida coast was my happy place.

There were no official markings on the jet, but as soon as I stepped inside, it was apparent this was a plane shared between the Boston hockey and football teams, as the logos were front and center, and the seats had fancy colored stitching.

Since I knew Sophie's biological father was a hockey player, I'd be wrong to dismiss what having a rich, famous parent could do for her. Money, houses, a different life from the one a struggling graphic artist could give her. And life.

Life was the important thing here. The chance for Sophie to have a first day at school, a first love, prom, college, maybe children of her own. Money wasn't important when life was the most precious thing of all.

"Mr. Bailey, welcome aboard," a woman greeted me and offered her hand. "Louisa James, Rebels hockey. Come this way."

I followed her to a group of seats, four that faced each

other, with a small table in between. Sophie was wide-eyed, cautious, but she allowed me to settle her in a seat and fasten her belt. She didn't want to let go of me fully as I awkwardly belted up and then leaned into her so she could hold my hand.

"Dadda?" she asked, which was her stock word for "what is happening, why am I here, explain it to me!"

"It's all okay, pumpkin," I whispered, then kissed her head.

"M'kay."

"She's a cutie," Louisa observed, and her smile was genuine. Sophie was a cutie, and I could see my sister in her smile.

"Thank you."

"So, I'll leave you alone, but if you need anything, I'll be near the front." She indicated to the cockpit where I could see the two pilots chatting. This wasn't like real life. This was unreal. "Snacks and drinks will arrive once we're in the air, but if little Sophie wants to run around, then it's a secure space here."

The rest of the flight passed in a complete blur. Sophie was intrigued, grumpy, sparky, then exhausted in the space of the three-plus hour flight, and sleeping was thankfully her current state as we landed. Her being asleep meant I could handle everything that was being thrown at us. There was another private car, only this time the driver didn't speak to me as he opened the door and I clambered in to find a booster seat already there. Instead, Louisa was talking to me—at me—and through all of this, I held Sophie's hand as she dozed. It turned out it wasn't just Sophie who needed to feel the touch.

"The Boston Rebels are pleased to welcome you to Boston," Louisa began and then went into the whole speech about the pedigree of the hockey team and integrity and trust, and then when she was finished, she handed me a file. "A standard NDA," she said. I took the folder before I realized what I was doing.

"Why do I need to sign this?"

She pursed her lips, then examined me thoughtfully. "It's for your and Sophie's protection. In this city, the Rebels are a big thing. The fact that one of our players has matched to Sophie has yet to hit the media, but when it does, you may find out to your detriment how passionate our fans can be." She was holding something back, so I opened the file, scanned the information, and noticed that it had several paragraphs on paternity along with secret-keeping.

"And this bit about paternal responsibility?"

"Protection for our team should you sue in a paternity case as this could become an unreasonable situation. It's standard wording in our NDAs."

I thrust the folder back. "My daughter is dying. I don't give a rat's ass about publicity or paternity. I want her to live. I won't tell anyone."

"It's considered that—"

"I won't be signing anything without a lawyer, and if this causes an issue, then I will force the position in the media myself. There's a match for Sophie, and that is all I'm here for."

"That's your choice."

Louisa nodded, and that was all we said for the remainder of the short journey to a private hospital. When we pulled up outside, she touched my arm as I moved to unbuckle Sophie.

"I do wish you and Sophie all the best, Isaac."

I thanked her because I was raised right, and then she guided me in through the wide front entrance and into the cool interior of a place nothing like I'd been in before. The clinic wasn't some vast place catering to the public. It had a calm and rarefied air to it, and the thick carpet made our footsteps whisper quiet. Where was the stark white, the people sitting waiting, the bustle of purpose?

Louisa led me straight past a receptionist who smiled at me and down a long corridor lined with photos that I assumed was Boston. I didn't know the city well, only that it wasn't Florida, and that was all that was important. Boston meant hope for Sophie, so it was the best place on Earth right now.

She opened a door and gestured for me to enter. I walked into the room and noticed a few sofas, a wide desk, windows with views of a landscaped garden, and standing in the middle of the room was a man so stunning that I wondered what I'd walked into. He was taller than me by a head, well over six feet, broad shoulders, wearing a suit and tie, and he was so pale that I thought he might keel over. His dark golden hair was neatly styled, a soft tumble of layers that had seen a better haircut than mine ever would, and he didn't move one inch, his mouth open and his eyes wide.

His dark hazel eyes.

No one had to tell me that this was Sophie's biological father. I could see it in his eyes and the shape of his face, but mainly in the shock and horror he had in his expression. He knew he'd had a baby with my sister, and it had hit him as hard as it hit me.

"Is that her?" he exclaimed, then went from pale to scarlet in an instant. "Sorry, I don't know what I'm supposed to say... Joachim Löfgren." I thought I detected an accent, but couldn't place it. European, I guess, although I wasn't an expert. He held out a hand, and we shook.

"Isaac Bailey," I replied, and as soon as we dropped hands, I took a few steps back from him.

"Is this... this..." He was at a loss for words, and I could see a hundred emotions churning in his expression. Shock was one of them. I would like to think I could see confusion and maybe sadness also, but was I projecting my own emotions onto him? For all I knew, he could be furious that he'd created a child with Ashley. He could start demanding to know why she hadn't told him or why she hadn't gotten rid of the baby. I didn't know him, and I didn't know what he was capable of.

"This is Sophie," I murmured and smiled down at her when she shifted in my arms, clearly fed up with being carried.

"Down, Dadda," she demanded, and *fuck*, I didn't want to let her go, but she'd spotted the toys in one corner, so how could I keep her from the toys. She wasn't interested in Joachim, and why would she be? He was just another stranger in her life that would pass through like so many others.

I went to a crouch, allowed her to slip from my hold, and she headed straight for the toys, her diapered butt a soft cushion as she went straight to the floor to pile bricks.

"Should she be doing that?" Joachim asked hurriedly. "What about germs, and I don't know, illness."

I could go into a long debate about why she wasn't isolated, about why her life was going along as usual until... *she left us.*

At first, I said nothing.

"She's fine," I said, and I sounded tired even to myself.

"I didn't know," he said after a moment's pause. *Here it comes, the dismissal of responsibility.* I waited for him to announce we could have his blood but that I shouldn't remind him he had a baby. I imagined we would be dismissed, then Sophie and I could get what we needed and go back to Florida.

He went to a crouch near her and picked up a teddy, making it dance in front of her.

"Hi, Sophie."

She side-eyed him, but the big man with the dancing bear couldn't pull her from the intense concentration needed for pushing a square brick in a round hole.

"Can she hear me?" he asked quickly, glancing up at me.

"She's not deaf. She has cancer," I snapped because hell, I was so confused by everything and worried, and this big hockey player was asking stupid questions. "Did no one tell you anything?"

"Yes, they did. I'm sorry. I don't mean..." He stood up and smoothed his suit pants, then shrugged. "I only found out two days ago, and it's a shock to know that I have a daughter. But you have to know that—"

"Will you do it?" I interrupted him.

He shot me a confused glance. "Sorry?"

"Will you go through with this procedure and try to save Sophie?"

His bewilderment cleared in a second, and he became focused and unwavering. He crossed his arms over his broad chest. "I'll do everything in my power to help Sophie. She can have *anything* she needs from me so that she can live."

I examined his expression, but there was no confusion or shock. There was only icy determination in his beautiful eyes, so like Sophie's, and I believed him.

"Okay."

He rolled his neck, dropped his stance, and held out a hand again.

"Between us, we'll work this out. Agreed?"

I didn't hesitate because this was Sophie, and she was my everything, so I shook his hand.

"Agreed."

Why did I feel as if I'd just made a deal with the devil?

Chapter Four

Joachim

IF EVER A MAN NEEDED AN AA MEETING, IT WAS NOW, AND
I was that man.

The time for hemming and hawing about finding a
group had passed when the word had come back that
not only was I a match for the sick little girl—Sophie
—but I was also genetically linked. The team had been
thrilled at first. What a marvelous PR coup! To have
the new guy—the known drunkard who was battling
the devil in a bottle in a new town—be a match for a
tiny little cherub battling cancer. The public relations
teams had probably creamed their shorts. Then they
found out that I'd impregnated a woman, left her in the
dust, and never once checked on her or the child that
I'd created. Not that I knew there had been a
pregnancy... oh, and that night that Sophie had been
conceived? I was drunk. Had to have been because I
had no recollection of the woman—Ashley—or the

night in question. Oh, and to boot, the woman had died while birthing the babe and her brother had taken over to raise the child.

Yeah, the PR people weren't quite so happy with me now. They could join the group. I wasn't pleased with me either. In fact, I was disgusted with me and the curdled legacy of my addiction. They were "spinning things" according to some young man with a tense set to his face when I'd met with them yesterday. Or had it been the day before? Fuck if I knew anymore. My life had been turned upside down. And I had yet to find a sponsor. The call of the gin bottle had been getting louder with each new and devastating announcement.

"… that will be the best way to handle this. What do you think, Joachim?"

I crashed back from the stratosphere at the sound of my name. I looked across the shiny walnut table the team had arranged for us to use in one of the conference rooms at Massachusetts Children's Hospital, which was where the transplant would take place. My agent Frank was staring at me, as were several pediatric oncologists, my attorney, surgeons, some lady from the hospital board, the team owner, Nick Sinclair, who for some ungodly reason had demanded to be present for all discussions, and Isaac. The girl—Sophie—was napping in Sinclair's lap, her head on his shoulder, clutching the stuffed Rebels mascot Eddie Eagle to her chest. Seemed my boss had a way with kids that I lacked. Sophie had warmed to him instantly. Me? Not so much.

"I'm sorry I missed what was said," I meekly confessed. Isaac was chewing on his thumbnail, his gaze darting steadily from his daughter… no, *my* daughter not his… my *daughter.* "Can you repeat what I missed?"

Frank, a tall man who resembled Liam Neeson minus the Irish accent, gave me his kindest smile. It was a farce of a smile. I'd seen that toothy grin appear right before Frank went in for the kill during negotiations with any team that I had played with. Guess Franklin Krensky was the closest thing to family that I had.

Not any more…

"It's fine, buddy, we know everyone is still a little dazed," Frank said, then reached out to pat me on the arm. Huh. That was above and beyond. Frank generally wasn't overly demonstrative, but perhaps he assumed we needed to put on a show for… who? The child? The attractive uncle? The team owner? "We were discussing where Mr. Bailey and his niece would be staying until the procedure in four days."

"Oh, I assumed they would stay with me. I've settled on a new house." I looked around the table, my gaze landing on Isaac. "It has a yellow ceiling that I plan to get painted. And the second bedroom is blue—the previous owners had sons—but I'm sure Sophie won't mind until I can contact a painter. It's on my to-do list."

I was supposed to call the painter three days ago. But somehow among the maelstrom that was my life now, I'd forgotten.

"No thank you. We'll stay in the hotel that the team has graciously provided," Isaac replied. I glanced to my lawyer, who shrugged. "Is that a problem? If the team isn't happy paying for the room, I can—"

"The team is thrilled to help financially in any way it

can. You don't have to worry about that, Mr. Bailey," Nick announced, then flashed the room that sleek, white smile of his. He then started talking about the Rebels and their donations to the hospital and the rooms that would be needed here for the child and me. Sophie. Damn it. Why was I having such trouble with making that paternal connection? I'd yearned for family for years now. Perhaps if I just stepped outside to get some air?

There was that bar we passed on Blossom Street. Just a short walk away. Some fresh air. A Tom Collins to calm your nerves and clear the cobwebs. What is one drink going to hurt? You've been through hell the past week, Loafy.

Loafy. Shit. How *dare* the devil inside my head use the nickname Moral had crowned me with just the other day? Fucker. The dirty fucker. A shudder of want coursed through me. I shot to my feet right in the middle of some speech one of the oncologists was making. My chair slammed into the brightly colored wall. Everything here was bright and happy. The walls, the floors, the ceilings. Everything but the sick children like Sophie. My daughter. Who was dying…

Everyone looked at me. I swiped at the cold sweat on my brow.

"I need some air. Excuse me, please." And with that, I bolted out the door to the nearest bank of elevators. I pounded on the G button with a mouth as dry as the Sahara, hands shaking steadily. Okay this was not good. I really needed to find a meeting before I did something stupid and—

"Mr. Löfgren, are you okay?" I spun from the lifts at

the sound of Isaac Bailey's strained voice. He was holding Sophie now, the little girl awake and smiling. At me. "Did I say something wrong? If you really want us to stay with you, we will, but I don't know you well and this is all so…" He floundered a bit.

"Yes, it's all that," I choked out. "All that and a bit more."

"Please don't leave. If you go, who will save Sophie?"

My gut cramped. I removed my hand from the panel of red buttons. My arm fell to my side.

"I'm not running from her. I would never do that. It was just…" I blew out a breath. How much about me did this man know? Should I tell him that I was freshly out of my fourth stint in rehab? Would he blanch or recoil as many did when they found out I was an alcoholic? Would he forbid me from seeing Sophie after the surgery? Suddenly the need to watch her grow and flourish seemed to be the most important thing in the world. For that to happen, I had to be honest about myself. I drew in a deep breath. "I was having a moment of weakness. I'm a recovering alcoholic and the past few days have been quite *auf den Kopf gestellt.*" He blinked at my German. "Topsy turvy." His big blue eyes fluttered nervously. Perhaps I had revealed too much. "If you're upset about my addiction…"

"No, I… no, of course not. Well, perhaps a little, but you're recovered, right?"

Sophie held out her eagle to me. "Kiss da bird."

A chuckle burst out of me as I took a step, then bent down to peck Eddie on his yellow beak. That made her laugh and something fundamental inside me unfurled like a flower opening to the sun. I'd never heard a sound as sweet as Sophie's laughter.

"I'll be recovering forever. I hope you won't hold that against me?" I asked Isaac as Sophie was dropping loud smacker kisses all over the Rebels mascot.

"If you won't hold it against me for keeping us in a hotel for a few days. You seem like a nice man, but I don't know you from Adam. I have to keep her safe."

"Of course, you do." I wanted to hug them both. Sophie for simply being Sophie and Isaac because… well, I wasn't sure why. Maybe to show him that I *was* a nice man. A weak man, yes, but a nice one. Perhaps I wished to hold him because he looked wan and terrified. Or maybe I simply wanted to feel the press of his lithe, hard body against mine. It had been many years since I'd been with a man. Women were simply easier to locate when one was a professional athlete. But this man… there was something about him that was wildly appealing. "Stay where you wish. My home will be open to you whenever you feel comfortable."

"Dadda, bird hunny," Sophie announced. Isaac nodded.

"The bird is hungry, which means that she's hungry," he explained.

"I read online that they have a wonderful cafeteria here. Would you like to get some lunch?" I offered. "My treat."

"Okay, thank you. We're kind of living off the generosity of strangers until I can get back to work," he shamefacedly explained.

"Work must come second to a child's health." I gave

him a smile, then had to kiss the bird again. "Let me tell them that we're taking a lunch break now."

"What if they get mad?" He glanced back at the door to the conference room.

I shrugged. "Then they'll get mad. My daughter is hungry."

Isaac stared up at me with round eyes filled with worry.

My daughter was hungry. And as her poppa, it was my place to feed her. Looking into eyes the exact same color as mine, I found a strength I wasn't aware of before. That of a parent who would do whatever was needed to protect his child.

His child. My child. My daughter...

LUNCH HAD BEEN QUITE THE EXPERIENCE. WE'D DINED ON chicken nuggets dipped in ketchup, tater tots dipped in ketchup, and pink milk, which I discovered was strawberry milk. I do not like strawberry milk I discovered, but it seemed that Sophie loved it. And ketchup.

Isaac had been withdrawn as we'd eaten. Which was understandable. His life was just as chaotic as mine was now, plus he had the burden of caring for a sick child. As we ate, I did the most talking, relaying about my life growing up in Switzerland, what it was like to move from the National League—which is the premier league in my home country—to the NHL where I'd played for Tampa Bay for many years. A shadow moved over Isaac's face when I spoke about Florida.

I hesitated to mention his sister still. How would I ever explain? When I'd been shown an image of the pretty young thing, there was no recognition at all. Which had made me sick with anger and regret. Which had led to me wishing I had a drink to dull the shame.

So that was why I was now sitting outside Faneuil Hall watching kids running by in tricorn hats while adults chattered on about the Trail of Freedom and waiting for the nearby Methodist Church to open its doors. There was an AA meeting in the basement at seven p.m., which I felt I had better attend. My demon had poked me twice today after being silent for quite a few months.

I scanned the crowds looking for a man. I'd spoken to the husband of the fellow I was to meet here and have sit by my side as I waded into my first group meeting. His name was Dan Arou, and he'd been an incredibly affable guy who talked at length about his own problems with painkillers when he'd been playing. I knew the name Arou well, as he'd just retired a year or so ago. As for his husband, well, I knew that name too. I caught the flash of bright red hair as the Venomous Pole weaved his way from the marketplace to me carrying two drinks in bright green cups.

"You stick out like a sore dick. Just saying that if you think you're incognito, you're not. I knew you were Joachim Löfgren a mile away and all the fans do too. You can't scam Boston sports fans. Trust me. I know from whence I speak," Victor Kalinski said as he dropped his lanky ass beside me on the city bench. Sighing heartily, I removed my Rebels cap and sunglasses. "Have an iced tea. It's not half bad. Not enough sugar, but I'm trying to cut back. Old man has diabetes and I'm fond of my toes. So, you're a drunk. Me too."

"Thank you." I took the drink from Vic and took a sip. It was cold, refreshing, and sadly lacking gin. "Your husband was very nice."

Vic smiled. "Yeah, he is. Everyone says he's a few bricks shy of a load to be hooked up with me." His gaze went skyward. I glanced upward and saw nothing but twilight settling over Boston. "Sometimes I wonder why he puts up with me, but then I recall that I have a massive dick, and it all makes sense." He jammed an elbow into my side and sniggered. "So, now that I broke the ice, tell me why you called for help. Been feeling the itch since you got out of rehab?"

"No, actually I had been doing well, but the past week has been..." I fumbled around for a fitting term.

"A shit fest of biblical proportions?"

I glanced at the man on my left. He had sharp hazel eyes and a long pointy nose that fit his long face well. His red hair gleamed copper and gold in the setting sun.

"That will do." I paused to sip and reflect. "Yes, that about covers it well."

"Yeah, we all have them wicked bad days. That's why we work the program." He poked at his drink with his straw. "Want to go into the particulars of your crappy week or do you just want to sit here and watch the seagulls shit on the tourists?"

"It wasn't so much that it was bad, it was just... intense." I wasn't sure how much I wanted to tell this man to be honest. I knew little about him other than he had played hockey for a bit and had retired after a brain injury.

Oh, and that he was an alcoholic. Like me. "I found out I had a daughter recently."

"Oh shit, yeah, that will stir up the hornets in your head."

I nodded, sipped my tea, and studied the cracks in the sidewalk. "I'd thought I was alone, but then this child appeared."

"So, this kid news really shook you, huh?"

"Deeply. She's sick. Leukemia. And she needs a bone marrow transplant, which I am one-hundred-percent ready and wanting to do!"

"Obvs."

"Yes, so it's not that I want anyone to think that I don't want to save my daughter's life because I do. It has just been a rush of things coming at me all at the same time. New team, new city, new home, and now a child. And her uncle."

"Yeah? Is he cute?"

I threw a confused look at Victor. "What? Why would you ask that?"

"Because you said the word 'uncle' like you were all up and ready to get into that." He shrugged, then took a loud slurpy sip of his tea. "Maybe I misread. So go on."

I stared at him for a long moment, then opted to simply dump it all on his lap. He'd signed up to be called by random drunks looking for help, right? So here I was. A random drunk looking for help. I talked and talked and talked. For hours it seemed, but in reality, only ten minutes had passed. When I ran out of steam after the meltdown at the elevator with the siren song of cold gin in my ears, I kind of stalled out like a broken Vespa.

"Wow, you really have had a ton of shit fall on your head. But hey, you did the right thing and reached out. And fuck but how lucky were you to get me?"

He gave me a wink that broke the tension of my purge. "Incredibly lucky."

"Damn straight. So, let's do this thing properly, shall we? The good Reverend has just opened the doors to the church, and I'm betting there's awful coffee and stale doughnuts waiting for us if we just leave this bench and walk down the block. What do you say?"

He stood up and looked down at me. I took a moment to gauge where I was mentally and found, to my amazement, that I felt a little lighter. And a bit more in control of my dark side. I'd never thought that simply talking to someone who had walked the same path I had would do so much good. Which was why I'd put off looking for a group here. The thought of people knowing me—and everyone here now knew me—and admitting what a fuck-up I was had sat wrong. But perhaps I simply needed a swift kick in the ass by fate to push me into admitting that I wasn't any better than the sanitation worker sweeping the street. I was a man with a problem that would not go away over time. I'd learned that in rehab, but had been reluctant to share my story with the world. But now I had to be strong. And sober. There was much more riding on my staying on the wagon than some bad press and a trade.

Now there was Sophie and Isaac who depended on me.

"Yeah, let's go have some bad coffee."

"That a man." Victor offered me his hand and I took it. "One day at a time, Jokey."

"Must you call me that?" I asked as he jerked me to my feet. It was worse than Loafy.

"Does it annoy you?"

"Yes, to be honest."

"Then that shall be your name forever more. Let's go. If you show up late, Carl eats all the chocolate doughnuts. What? Don't fucking judge me. I bought the unsweetened tea, didn't I?"

Boston was turning out to be a unique and boisterous town filled with surprises. Some good, some bad, and some life-altering.

Chapter Five

Isaac

MY DAUGHTER.

The words followed me out of that meeting and back to my hotel room, where I sat in absolute silence rocking a fretful Sophie and replaying every syllable on repeat.

"I had to know this could happen. He's your daddy by blood." She blinked up at me, her dark eyes wide at the sound of my voice.

"Dadda," she murmured and curled her hand around mine. She was fighting sleep, and for the longest time, I stared down at her, seeing the shape of her mom's face, the long lashes, the way her curls were damp with exertion from crying.

She *was* my daughter. Not in-law. I was *only* her uncle, but she was my daughter by heart. *My daughter*. But that's what Joachim had said, and he had more of that claim than I ever could.

My daughter.

The words had dripped with emotion as if something had clicked into place, and his shock had given way to a warrior's purpose. I knew without a doubt that, from that moment on, he would put Sophie's life above his. Wasn't that all I wanted? I refused to think that I could lose her. Ashley had given her to me. I was her uncle, and I couldn't think about tomorrows when todays were so hard.

Finally, Sophie's eyes stayed closed, and her breathing settled.

"Love you, Sophie-boo," I whispered, then waited a few moments to see if she would remain asleep before I tiptoed out of the bedroom. Even though I knew I'd hear her with the door closed—I'd become very good at waking in an instant if she needed me—I left her door open enough so I could see her from the sitting area. The Rebels hadn't just given me a motel room, nope, this was a penthouse suite in a hotel that screamed luxury. It had two bedrooms, a marble bathroom, sitting room, and kitchen, not to mention a huge flatscreen TV and spectacular views over the city and harbor that blew my artist's mind. Two doors opened to a patio area with a table. I was drawn to it, though I didn't step outside.

Deciding to grab the quickest shower on record, I changed out of my pants and shirt, and stepped into the spa-like shower. When I was finished, I put on my PJs and headed into the kitchen for a drink. The small kitchen had two cupboards, and each was packed with coffee, tea, cocoa, and snacks, and on the counter, there was a big bowl of fruit. What I *should* have done is have a glass of water, an apple, and head to bed, but it was only eight and still daylight outside the window, plus I had work to catch up on.

Instead, I made a hot chocolate and curled up on the vast sofa with my traveling art kit. I'd become an expert in working for clients, or for myself, in the weirdest of places. Sitting in the hospital or curled on the floor next to Sophie's crib at home, even in the car waiting for results. Art was my income, graphics for clients, but my private art was where I hid my pain—safely locked away in slashes of black and gray.

"What now?" I asked my sketchbook, then sipped at the smooth chocolatey goodness until the warmth of it began to curl inside me. Glancing around me for inspiration, I felt a hint of an idea.

When he had accompanied me to the room, the manager had apologized that I didn't have a private pool. I could have joked that I wasn't the swimming pool kind of boy, given I'd grown up in the Keys and the ocean was my home, but I sensed this was very important to him, and never let it be said I wasn't good at making other people feel better. Anyway, if I'd said something like that, I genuinely think he'd have a breakdown because he was already concerned that the crib wasn't big enough for Sophie and that he hadn't thought to buy some children's toys. I'd stayed in a lot of hotels since Sophie became part of my life, and not once had there been toys in the room, and the crib was more a full-size bed with rails.

This suite was a palace compared to some of the motels, but it was just as impersonal, and it wasn't home. I picked up a black marker and drew thick black lines for this week's comic strip. Wilma Payne was my alter ego, the drawings that I created for *me*, commenting on grief, fears, social issues, politics, inequality, anything I felt that I wanted to make a statement about. I poured my restless angsty heartbroken heart into this art that was available free on a ton of different platforms.

I tapped my pen on my knee, going over every moment of today but it was too big to capture in a few strokes. I decided to focus on the room and the ridiculousness of someone like me being in a suite like this. The space was elegant as if it was a millionaire's lair, complete with a balcony that was all very action hero inspired, like Batman, with carved gargoyles on the corners. I was in my happy place, quite at peace, as I drew a superhero with a large M on his chest, complete with cape, standing on the balcony, the wind tugging at his cape.

"Ladies and gentlemen, I give you Millionaire Man!" I announced to the empty room and winced in case I'd woken up Sophie. There was no sound from her room, but I checked in there anyway, and then it was back to the cartoon. I had Millionaire Man lamenting that his life was destroyed because there was no swimming pool in his penthouse, and in the next scene, had a single tear running down his face over the fact the coffee wasn't fresh. In the last frame, his anguished expression over the wrong kind of snacks was way too close to home, and I realized I'd unintentionally drawn a reflection of what I felt.

I wish my thoughts were as simple as missing pools and the wrong kind of snacks.

With the preliminary sketch done, I turned to my iPad to create the real version for uploading, but a soft knock on the door pulled me from my safe world of art. Fear made my heart stop when I saw Joachim through the peephole. Had I misjudged him? Was he here to tell me he'd changed his mind? I yanked open the door prepared to do anything to get him to help Sophie.

"You have to help us, please," I demanded and begged before he could even get a smile in, and his eyes widened.

"I am. I will. I just thought I'd check in, and uhm, I get it's late." He stared down at his hands, the confident determined man who'd called Sophie his daughter was nervous, and compassion pushed aside my fear and the surge of adrenaline ebbed away leaving me shaky and confused. "Can we talk?" He hesitated. "I don't have to come in if you're..." He waved at my PJs, and I shook my head. I didn't care what I was wearing right now, I was in relieved mode, and hell, since Sophie came into my life, if anyone visited me past the magic evening hour of eight, then they should expect me to be getting ready for bed. I took every single second of Sophie sleeping to at least chill, even if I couldn't get my own sleep in.

"No, come in. It's fine. Just talk quietly because Sophie's sleeping."

"Can I see her? Not wake her up, just look at her?"

Again, he was so uncertain, but I led him to the room because I couldn't deny him access to his daughter even if I was torn between needing him for her and not wanting him anywhere near her.

He stood at the end of the large crib, and the room shrank around us with the big hockey player hovering. His hands pushed into his jeans, his big shoulders hunched, and I'd never seen such confusion in a person before.

"Is she okay?" he whispered.

I nodded, then indicated we needed to leave before talking. He was new to this parenting thing, and he had to learn that sometimes you had to let a sleeping baby lie.

"She's fretting some, but she's at least sleeping," I explained as we ended up by the two sofas in the sitting area. I gathered up all my art things and shoved them in the messenger bag, and in all that time, Joachim hadn't moved, just stared out the window in a daze.

"I have this whole list of questions…" He closed his eyes and took a deep breath, letting it out slowly. "Things that she's feeling. Pain, bruising, infections, fevers, what symptoms does she have? Does she have them all? Is it me? Is it my fault? Did I do this to her?"

The visible spiraling was senseless as all the words spilled out, and I pressed a hand to his chest. "Sit down."

He blinked at me as if he hadn't heard me right. After a moment, he slumped into the sofa as if strings had been cut.

"Sorry," he muttered.

"Can I get you a coffee or something? Hot chocolate?"

"Water is fine. I didn't mean to interrupt."

I found a bottle of water in the packed refrigerator and passed it to him before retaking my seat on the sofa and nursing my hot chocolate. He deserved to hear it all. After all, he was Sophie's baby daddy, but whereas I'd learned the overall picture in small doses with time to process, I was going to have to lay everything on him all in one go. One of the small marshmallows bumped my nose as I licked the cream. I caught it with my tongue and sighed as it melted in my mouth. I heard a noise, but it was just Joachim coughing. Now it was time to concentrate.

"Where do you need me to start?"

He wriggled to sit upright and toyed with the label on his bottle, not quite meeting my gaze.

"When did you know?"

That was the hardest of all questions. "I was so new—I mean new at looking after a baby—so maybe I overreacted a few times to innocent things, and I guess that was a lucky thing. She was tired, lethargic, there were bruises, and her belly seemed hard. I took her to the ER, and then everything was out of my hands. They did all kinds of tests, but I recall, through all of them, she was just exhausted. They told me she had B-cell acute lymphocytic leukemia. I didn't know what to do or say. I mean, I'd lost her mom, and I was caring for her and somehow on my watch she'd become ill."

"None of this is your fault," he blurted, but he didn't know what he was saying. Mom and Dad had died because Ashley and I were supposed to be watching our pet terrier, and I'd been too scared, and our parents looked for him just to stop us crying, and they'd never made it to shelter. Even counselling couldn't completely strip me of guilt.

Then Ashley had passed when I had hold of her hand. I couldn't save any of them, and I might not be able to save Sophie either. I had come to a point in my life where I felt cursed.

"Her outlook is good as long as she gets the stem cells from your blood to balance the chemo."

He went white, bent over, his elbows on his knees, his head hanging, and something compelled me to touch him. Reassurance cost nothing, and I'd had a lot of touches from a hundred nurses and doctors. Every single touch was a mark of hope on my skin, and he *needed* that. He glanced at me then down at my hand on his forearm, and I squeezed quickly before moving back. Sometimes there was no need for words.

"I can't imagine… she's so little," he whispered, and my chest tightened.

"You can save her," I murmured and edged away from him into my corner of the sofa, pulling up my legs and encircling them with my arms. For the first time, I got a real look at the man who'd been part of making Sophie. He was a classic professional jock, all muscles and power, but he looked like a broken man right now, and compassion swelled inside me.

"I want to save her. I want to know her." He glanced at me, and there was a sincerity in his gaze that I believed completely. "She deserves to have her dad in her life."

"She calls me Dad," I reminded him.

"Of course she does." He tripped over himself with the speed those words came out. "You're her uncle and you're all she's known. I get that. But we could be Dad and Uncle for her, and when she's older she'll have both of us."

Hope bloomed in my chest. He wasn't demanding anything from me, not taking over, although he had the biological right to make decisions for Sophie. What if he'd been religious and didn't believe in intervention? What if he'd died? What if… what if he wanted to take her from me?

If he saves her life, then I don't care.

For months, I'd cried from losing my parents, my grief magnified by the media who circled the tragedy of Hurricane Wilma like vultures. For days, I'd cried for

Ashley as I held her hand and willed her to live, wondering how I'd ever come to terms with being alone. Then when they told me about Sophie, I allowed myself an hour of anger, horror, and grief, and decided that for her, I had to rise above all of that and not let the grief at a bleak future consume me. My life mantra was that I'll find a way to cross bridges when I reach them.

Joachim was a bridge. That was all.

"Do you like it here?" he asked, and I was thrown for a moment.

"It's a nice suite," I said.

"I've spent a lot of time in hotels when I've been playing." He sighed. "Hockey I mean."

"I know what you meant."

"They're not home." He stared out the window again. "I have two spare rooms, a yard, and I'm close to water. It's not much. I'm not... I don't have a lot left from before, addiction breeds addiction, and I lost most of it." He grimaced, burying his face in his hands. "But I earn good money. I'll pay for anything she needs, and I would love it if you decided to come and live in my place, so I can get to know my daughter properly. I have a car you can use, and I've already opened an account for you and her, so you have money. It's not paying you or anything, there's no catch, although the Rebels' lawyer is having kittens. I don't care about all of that. Please move into my home. Even though it's not much, it's a cool place, and you'd have it to yourself most of the time. I won't be around much when I'm training and playing... if I can play." He turned to face me. "I need to have an injection of a growth factor."

That was a quick switch in conversation. "G-CSF," I confirmed. The drug was to encourage the stem cells to move from the bone marrow into the blood, and he would need injections for a few days leading up to the collection, which was penciled in with a date already.

"Yeah, the doctor said it mobilizes the stem cells. The Rebels' doctor is working with the donor team, and I went to an AA meeting today. So, please can I get to know Sophie? Will you come home with me?"

I waited for more, but clearly, he'd finally run out of the arguments he'd obviously rehearsed before he got here.

"You went to an AA meeting?"

"Yeah, I have a sponsor. He's a retired hockey player who won't take any shit. I hit rock bottom, and I know you don't know me from Adam, but I want to work the steps for myself, make myself whole again, learn to live with the addiction, and be a good dad for Sophie."

I needed to do research on AA because I was sure there were rules about forming attachments or was that just to other addicts? He didn't say he was sober only for Sophie, he said he was working to be sober so he could be there for her. My heart hurt for him, and for Sophie, and I didn't want to be in a hotel, not really.

Maybe he'd shown me enough honesty for me to trust him, and I should trust my instincts. He was so earnest, *handsome*. I couldn't help my libido. I'd always been attracted to jocks with their focus and strength, but it wasn't that part of my body that spoke for me right now.

It was my heart.

"Come and pick us up in the morning. We'll be ready."

And his smile was a beautiful, peaceful thing.

Chapter Six

Joachim

It was amazing what a little cash and a well-known name could do.

By eight o'clock the next morning there were painters in my house. Two teams. One was fixing that terrible yellow living room ceiling—and freshening up the walls with some eggshell white—and the other was giving the blue bedroom a new coat of pale cream. As they scurried around throwing drop cloths onto the floor, I knocked back a protein shake and some scrambled eggs with rye toast with haste. I had morning skate to attend to first off, and then I was to pick up Isaac and Sophie at eleven. To bring them home. To my home. My daughter and her cute uncle.

It was kind of silly how bubbly with excitement my stomach was. Today was a big day, and while I knew I was riding a high, I also had to keep life in perspective. For every sunny day, there were rainy ones. Life was all about finding and maintaining that balance. I made a note in my online day planner to attend a meeting tonight, then I left the house in the capable hands of the painters that Xander had recommended. The Rebels chatroom was a true lifesaver.

As I drove to the barn, my radio was set to a talk radio show where the people had such thick Boston accents, I had trouble deciphering some of what they were saying, my thoughts went to Xander and Brady. This morning, we were choosing a new team captain. I felt oddly out of sorts being asked to participate in the selection. I'd been here for a month, had played four preseason games, and had finally gotten the nametag over my cubicle spelled correctly. Someone kept forgetting the umlaut over the O in my last name. I wasn't sure a player who had just gotten his umlaut should be picking the captain, but the team had insisted. It felt off to me to pick the replacement for the man I had replaced. But that was hockey. And I was lucky to have been given this second chance. To be fair it was more like a tenth or eleventh chance given all my issues over the years. Tampa Bay had been extremely understanding for many years but even they had reached the end of their rope with me and my addiction problems. Which was also totally justified.

What I knew of either man was limited to ice time and a few social gatherings, such as awards and fundraisers. The old captain, Brady Rowe, had always been an upstanding man both on and off the ice. His brother Jamie spoke well of him in the locker room back down in Tampa, and the family was hockey through and through. Xander was an enjoyable sort, calm and cool, always willing to talk to his teammates and offer advice.

Parking in my appointed slot next to Marquis and his sleek new red Jaguar, I stared at the rink as the morning sun glinted off the mirrored sides. Was there anything prettier than a hockey rink?

Your daughter.

"Okay, yes, true." With a smile on my face, I hustled into the players' entrance, took a moment to speak with the security guard at the door, and then was swooped down upon by the team owner, who was wearing a white linen shirt, tan pants, and a hat with a wide white band.

"There you are!" Nick shouted and several heads turned. I gave Renco and Austin a confused look as Sinclair threw an arm around my shoulder. Or tried. He wasn't quite as blessed in the height department as I was. "So how are we feeling? Good? Any side effects from the super solider serum they're giving you?"

"I, uhm… the injections start—"

"Good! Good. Listen… can you hunker down a bit? There you go. So, I have a favor to ask of you. Rumor has it that your daughter and her uncle are moving into your house."

He waved his left hand as he spoke. His cologne was musky and expensive, not unpleasant, but not nearly as appealing as the fresh scent that Isaac wore.

I threw a look over my shoulder at the two young guys playing soccer in the corridor. Austin blushed pink and turned his head just as Renco booted the ball to him. It bounced off his head, and he fell with a grunt.

"He'll be fine," Nick said as he led me along by my neck. "So, is your daughter moving in?"

"Yes, that's true. How did you—"

"Never mind how. I have ears all over this place. There's nothing that happens on my team that I don't know about." He gave me a wink. "Right, so, this favor I have is a small one, but could give big rewards. You want the team to look good, right?"

"Sure, yes, of course."

"Excellent!" His teeth flashed white against his olive complexion. "So, here's what we're going to do. I'm sending a PR team with some local media to your house to capture the heartwarming moment that your precious, but sickly, daughter moves into your home."

I stalled like a flooded engine. "I'm not sure that having people there will be a good thing."

"Of course, it will! Joachim, this story is big. Huge! Every network from here to Moose Cranny, Manitoba wants some time with you and precious Sophie. Can you blame them? What a heartwarming story. It's like a Hallmark movie come to life. If only it were Christmas…"

"No," I said with determination.

"Huh?" Nick.

"No cameras."

"For real?"

"Really. No cameras when they move in."

"Okay. This time." Then he drifted off wearing a dreamy expression. "Anyway." He snapped back, then began walking me along again. "The point is that this story is massive. And it's only going to get bigger and bigger as we progress through the treatments. Which is why we need to get on this now, and push it big and hard. To that end, and I know you'll be thrilled, I went right to the top of the

Boston news channels. Guess who's going to do the interview?"

"I'm not sure…"

"Belinda Berks!" I blinked down at him. His dark eyes rolled. "Belinda Berks! She's the anchor for *WBOS Action News at Six*. Really? Do you not watch TV?"

"Some. Nature shows mostly, although I do enjoy a good murder mystery."

He turned to look at me, his hand resting on the back of my neck. "Focus here, Joachim. This is the biggest story this city has seen since Paul Revere rode through town yelling about the British. Hell, this could be the biggest story to ever come out of Boston! Bigger than the tea party!"

I was beginning to think that Nick was prone to exaggeration. "I'm not sure—"

"Well, I am. If there's one thing I know how to do it's selling things. Olive oil, carpets, stocks, bonds, sports teams, stories. You just leave it all with me and, within a week, the people of this glorious city will have forgotten that you're a man with a checkered past and will be nominating you for sainthood." He lifted the Greek Orthodox cross that hung around his neck and kissed it.

"I'm just not sure—"

"Good! Here we are. In you go. Time to vote." He shoved me into the locker room, then hustled off as if he were on a mission from God.

"Loafy! Stop dawdling out there. Get in here!" Moral bellowed, then sauntered past in just his jockstrap and a feather boa. Both were pink. I didn't ask. The entire team was present, including Xander, who looked as if he were trying to digest something squirmy. I sat down in front of my cubicle, smiled at the umlaut, and then fell into silence. It felt like a high holy moment as Austin, because he was the youngest and tended to get the grunt jobs, handed out slips of paper and stubby pencils to each man.

"The reason we use this method is to remind us of our heritage," Xander announced as Austin made his way around the oval room. "This is how the first Boston captain, Andre St. Price, was chosen back in 1928. Paper and pencil, then the names are dropped into the stein used by Carl 'Cracker' Mills who was the first starting goalie."

Renco stood up, an old beer stein in his hand, and began following Austin. No one spoke as they wrote down the name of the man they felt would represent them the best. I jotted down Xander's name, folded my scrap of paper, and waited for Renco. He gave me a smile as I shoved my vote into the cracked ceramic stein with an even older Rebels logo on the side. He was a cute kid. Intense on the ice, as most goalies were. Pleasant, but incredibly withdrawn, which could also be attributed to being a goalie. They were a unique bunch. After all the votes had been cast, Renco carried the stein over to Moral who, for some reason unknown to me—perhaps it was the pink boa and jockstrap—began counting each vote and marking each pick on a chalkboard that hung on the wall. Every man in the room was as quiet as if they were in church. I watched the tally rise for Xander. When all was said and done there was only one vote not for Xander, but for one of the other alternates. I had to assume that was Xander's vote, as he struck me as a humble man. But then most hockey players were. Moral stood up.

"The team has chosen Xander Holden as captain," Moral announced and the team, as one, rose to their feet to cheer for their new captain. Xander got a little choked up but managed to cough out a short little "thank you and I promise to do my best for the team and each of you" type of speech. Then he told us all to get our asses on the ice, aside from Moral who really needed some padding before he laced the skates. We all laughed at that, none louder than the big ginger with the bushy beard.

"Congratulations," I said to Xander after the mad rush at his stall had cleared a bit.

"Thank you." He grasped my hand and shook it.

"How does it feel to be the first out captain?"

"It's fine. No pressure or anything." He made a sickly face, then gave me a swat on the shoulder. "Do you need any help getting your girl moved into your place?"

And that right there was why some men were born captains. He could have basked in his achievement—and it was a huge one—but instead he was worrying about others on the team. Even though I didn't know Xander well, I was happy with the vote I'd cast.

"Nope, they don't have much," I said and felt some sadness for their circumstances. Now that they were with me, I'd make sure my daughter was well provided for. Which was why I was speaking to a lawyer. It might take some time, but I needed to ensure that Sophie was legally listed as my child. I also wanted the world to know that she was my daughter and that her dad was taking care of her as only a father could.

I WAS RUNNING LATE TO PICK UP SOPHIE AND ISAAC. NICK had set up some sort of presser for me. The lady who met me beside the ice was nice and pretty, but her questions were centered more on how I could have fathered a child and not known. I did my best to remain polite, but when she started getting aggressive, Nick flew in, smile in place, and led her off to have lunch with him in the owner's box. She kept throwing dirty looks my way as she was steered down the chute from the ice.

"Wow, that was intense," Moral commented as he skated up with a bucket of pucks that he'd had to pick up after practice. His punishment for flashing his pink jock strap at Renco to fluster the poor kid so he could sneak a goal past him. It had worked. Then he'd been whistled down by Coach and placed on clean-up duty. "Want to help collect cones?"

"Sorry, no, I have to pick up my daughter, and I'm already behind."

"Go get your girl. I'll rope Rowe into helping. *Hey, Peachy!*" He bellowed as he went off to find Austin. Smiling at the antics that took place here, I rushed through my shower, skipping the razor, and jumped into my rental. While I missed my Porsche, it turned out to have been serendipitous that I'd sold it. I was a family man now. Which meant I'd need a family-type car. Maybe one of those SUVs with the screens in the back of the front seats. I bet Sophie would like that. Grinning like a fool, my head filled with ideas for my next car purchase, I pulled up in front of the hotel that was housing my newfound kin. I dashed into the lobby and into the nearest elevator.

As I rode up, I contemplated the changes that had

taken place in my life. There had been so many, all rather large, and yet here I was, going on three months sober. My daughter and… the doors opened to let an older couple in. I smiled and smashed myself against the wall as the man and woman continued their conversation about boating. So exactly what was Isaac to me? Not exactly my brother-in-law because I'd not married his sister. He was simply my daughter's loving uncle and caretaker. And he was adorable to boot.

When I rapped on the door, he opened it and his expression was not adorable.

"You're late," he informed me. I nodded sadly. Seemed Isaac was not a fan of being tardy.

"I'm sorry. I should have texted. I'm really garbage about contacting people. I'm not used to answering to others and I just forget." He didn't appear to be much swayed. "The owner had some reporter come in for an ice-side interview that didn't go well."

"I understand," he said, but I wasn't sure that I was that easily forgiven. "We're ready to go. Just let me grab our bags."

"Ring for the porter," I said, stepping into the luxury suite just as Sophie looked up from a coloring book. She gave me a timid smile that made my belly feel as if there were a flock of butterflies trying to burst free.

"Oh, I'm not sure if we need to bother him." I sat down next to Sophie as Isaac began hoisting bags to his shoulders.

"It's his job," I replied, then asked my daughter what she was coloring.

"A cow," she informed me as she continued to fill in the entire page with a blue crayon.

"I love blue cows," I said, which got me another smile. "Are you ready to move in with me? I have a new room painted just for you!"

"I ready!" She threw down the crayon and climbed into my arms. I cradled her close, inhaling the sweet scent of baby shampoo on her hair. She weighed less than nothing. "You have a pokey face." She patted my scruffy cheeks, and I laughed at her candor.

I dropped a kiss to her warm brow as my gaze met Isaac's. It was impossible to guess what he was thinking, but not what he was feeling. I could see worry and apprehension in his gaze. Which I fully understood. He didn't know me at all, and yet, he had put all his trust in me. I would not let him or my baby girl down. He didn't have to worry about that.

"I'll take care of her," I whispered, and he nodded, but the concern lingered in his blue eyes. Perhaps it would take more than a weak promise from an ex-drunk to convince him, and rightfully so. I'd go above and beyond to show him that I could be the father Sophie needed and deserved. Once we had the medical issues behind us, our lives would be sunshine and applesauce, as my grandmother used to say. Sophie would grow up to be big and strong and incredibly smart. Isaac could return to the life he had before he'd been called into being a caregiver for my daughter. Hell, perhaps he could stay here in Boston. Maybe we could explore this spark of attraction between us. The world was full of glorious possibilities now that Sophie was part of my existence.

Chapter Seven

Isaac

He was holding Sophie, and I hated it.

Fear burned in my gut because this huge, rough hockey player with all his issues picked up my daughter… niece… as if he had every right to do that. Which he did. Which made me miserable, angry, contented, hopeful, angsty, and fuck knows what else, all at the same time. Not to mention he'd been late for whatever ridiculous reason he'd tried to hand me, which I couldn't come to terms with because my life with Sophie was regimented to the minute, and I'd been disappointed when he hadn't arrived the very second that I'd been ready for him. Hell, *he* should be running on my and Sophie's schedule, not the other way around. We were packed. Sophie was coloring in a comic book I'd created for her, and I'd made sure that all my defenses were in place, settled into how I was going to handle him showing up. Then he hadn't arrived, and I'd had too much time to worry about all the things that could go wrong with what we were doing. I wavered between staying and going, and I even unpacked my case once, only to shove everything back in when I realized I was being dumb. But there were all these questions in my head.

He was holding Sophie, and I loved it.

Seeing Sophie cradled in his arms, knowing he was saving her life, was the most heroic image I'd ever seen, something that would inspire any superhero, and my artist's eye wanted to capture him in bold strokes that portrayed his strength, and his confusion, but also his determination to do what was right.

I followed him to the elevator, the case I was tugging caught on the door, and I held out a hand to stop him from helping me because I was perfectly capable of carrying all this stuff in one go.

"We should have called someone to help us with the cases," he chided softly, and I glared at him, but he wasn't looking at me. He was staring down at Sophie with such a look of wonder in his expression that I couldn't bring myself to say anything. Sophie deserved this quiet moment where everything was okay. When the doors shut, she tipped her head and stared at Joachim and then over to me with a wide smile. She must be feeling good, rested after getting a couple of hours sleep. I envied that Joachim was seeing her at her absolute best, when she wasn't in pain, when her belly wasn't bloated, and when her eyes weren't screwed up in tears. I'd seen good times, but I'd been present for so many bad moments. That must be why I was feeling possessive until guilt flooded me because I shouldn't be thinking negatively about Sophie being well. His hazel eyes brimmed with something akin to awe, and he didn't say anything until we left by a back door, walking to the car, which he'd parked a short stroll from the hotel. He'd taken one of the cases from me, hefting it as if it weighed nothing, and I followed on behind, sure that he could carry all three in one hand, plus Sophie, plus the burden of everything that had changed for him.

Competent. Capable. Strong. Determined. Fighting his demons.

Sexy.

Sexy?

That was not what I should be focusing on, but I couldn't help it because my uneasy thoughts made me desperate for something else to latch onto. Not to mention I'd filled the time while waiting for him this morning, irritated, checking out Google articles that would tell me he was a waste of space whom I shouldn't trust.

Yes, there'd been stories of rehab, Instagram meltdowns, arguments at his old team, but a lot of what was posted was balanced by how he played. Whatever the demons, he was clearly good at his job. A career I knew very little about, only that it was hockey, and he was a defenseman. Pundits said that for all his issues, he was a good player, as if that excused the drinking and acting out. Too often professional sports had a toxic environment where a player was given too much leeway as long as they performed for the team.

I wondered, if his team had called him on his shit and held him accountable, whether he wouldn't have carried on with the drinking. *As if I know what I'm talking about. Armchair psychology for the win.*

All I know is that he was different than the man I

expected from the descriptions in Ashley's journal because the picture she'd created of him was very sparce and I'd filled in the gaps.

Hockey Guy to me was more than likely an asshole, probably married, a failed college jock who worked in an office, and relived his glory days in random bars. Although some of that was me projecting all the negative jock stereotypes I could onto the nameless faceless man who'd created a baby without even knowing about it.

Ashley had described her hookup as a party dude, prone to drinking more than he could hold, sleeping around, *a player*, but she never explicitly gave me names. All I knew is what she'd told me. He meant nothing to her, but her workmates had bet her she couldn't land him. By the time I'd even gotten that small amount of information out of her, she'd been seven months pregnant and already showing signs of the pre-eclampsia that would ultimately steal her from Sophie's life, and mine.

I wish she had told me more because if I'd known about him as a person and not just a code in a journal, I would have found him. Maybe he could have been with Ashley and then maybe my sister might not have died.

I needed to remember that fate or the gods or whoever was out there controlling this mindfuck that was life had never given me a chance to do anything. None of this was my fault, but I'd chosen to stay with Sophie. I'd handed my heart to her wrapped in ribbons. If she didn't live, then what was left of me? What was I without her?

Frozen in place, my chest tightened, and my vision blurred, and I dropped my hold on the cases.

"Isaac?" I heard my name, but it echoed strangely, and

everything was gray and blurry. Joachim murmured words, patted my shoulder, and I knew I should say something to acknowledge him, but nothing was happening. "It's okay, Isaac, let's get these in the car, come on, sit down."

"I'm fine," I lied and blinked my way back to reality. He was still holding Sophie, staring at me as if I was a bug on display.

"Isaac—"

"It's okay." I bent to pick up the cases, realizing that put me right at the level of his ass as he turned to buckle Sophie into a car seat.

I appreciated the form of the man who was holding Sophie. Jeans molded strong thighs, and a butt that could fuel my fantasies for a while, not to mention his shirt strained whenever he flexed his biceps. *Fuck my life he's hot.* Was it inappropriate to balance my worries with admiring his ass? I could admire, right? It wasn't as if I wanted anything to come of it because Sophie was my focus, but it didn't hurt to look. What am I doing? I bet he could pick me up, throw me over his shoulder, and—

"Are you okay?" he asked as he popped the trunk.

"Huh?"

"You look pale, are you okay?" He frowned but I wasn't going to explain the thought processes that had traveled through me a hell of a long way in a few minutes of silence.

"I'm fine."

He gave me a crooked, but uncertain, smile and by the time the bags were in Joachim's rental, I'd forced my worries, fears, panic, and untimely attraction into a box and gone back to focusing on what happened next.

It was forty minutes of silence as we drove out of the city and headed to the borough of Dedham, to the address he'd given on the medical records. The house itself was small but sturdy, opposite Wigwam Pond, whatever that was, and something about it made me feel instantly happy. Nothing like I expected. It wasn't some huge millionaire's mansion, but rather it was homey with a front yard. Only I couldn't see all of it because it was blocked by two white vans and a truck, and there were sawhorses on the small patch of grass.

"They said they'd get everyone on this so it will be done by the end of today," Joachim explained, wincing at me and glancing at Sophie, who clung to my neck wide-eyed and open-mouthed. "I didn't think this through," he muttered.

"Are they rebuilding your house from the foundation up?" I asked with care, worrying that the idea of staying with Joachim to give Sophie time with her father was going to cause issues.

"No, I promise it's not as bad as it looks. They have this many guys so they can do it fast, but I didn't expect so *much.*"

I went into instant caretaker mode—my default setting —and pressed a kiss to Sophie's forehead then smiled at him.

"We're up for an adventure, but can we at least find a quiet spot, away from the workers?"

His lips pursed in thought, and then he grinned. "Yes, follow me." He walked away from the car and snapped his fingers. "Shoot. Bags." As easy as if they were anti-gravity cases, he had all three, plus my backpack, and juggled them to shut the trunk. "Follow me."

He led us around the side of the house and gestured us through an open gate before kicking it shut behind us. Then down a short path through the yard, passing untamed bushes, until finally it opened out and there was a brand-new wooden structure. A shed only fancier.

"I was going to use this for gym equipment, but actually it would make a cool playhouse, right?" He opened the door with a flourish as if he was showing us a palace.

Sophie had a playhouse, made of plastic, in the corner of her room, but it was nothing like what this could be with beanbags and toys, a sofa maybe, bookcases, all of that, and it could be the absolute best thing for her.

Better than her tiny bedroom back home.

I needed to stop overthinking about this. It's a shed for God's sake.

"Stay here," he instructed, and still with the cases in hand, he jogged to the house, disappearing inside. Jogged. With three cases. Muscles bunched as he jumped the step inside, and then nothing happened for five minutes.

"Just you and me then, Sophie."

"Want down, Daddy," she demanded, and I went to a crouch as she clambered from my hold and explored the space. It was big, maybe fifteen by fifteen, glass in the ceiling, solid, the kind of place that was a step up from storing a lawnmower, and I could see it had both plumbing and electric. There was a large cardboard box in a corner and Sophie was up on tiptoes and peering in. I went to her side immediately in case there were things in there that she shouldn't be touching, but the box was empty. The two of us tilted it on its side, and she crawled in. "My new house," she exclaimed and sat down looking as pleased as any small kid with a box.

A commotion at the door made me glance back, and I did a double take when I saw a whole line of people was carrying furniture. There was a large sofa, a separate chair, a small table, boxes of other things, a rug, a TV, a laptop, even a planter.

"What's this?"

"We shouldn't go into the house for a few hours, so I brought the house out here. Is that okay? For Sophie, I mean." He held up a hand to stop two brawny guys covered in paint from muscling the sofa in.

"For Sophie?"

"Do we need to disinfect things? I should have thought of that, what if—"

"It's all good." I kept an eye on it all as the furniture was fitted in snuggly and Sophie sat in the box and peered at everything going on.

"Thanks, guys," Joachim said. As they left, he chatted with them, giving them fist bumps and selfies, and he even allowed one of the women to kiss him on his cheek *for luck*. Who were these people to him? They seemed very accommodating for general builders and decorators. "Sorry about that," he leaned against the closed door, "everyone thinks they know me." He shrugged, but the words were weighty with meaning—I just couldn't figure out if he was angry or happy that he was the center of attention.

"You didn't need to do this," I began, but he waved it away.

"My daughter needs space, then I make space. Everything I can fix I will do," he added, grinning back at me. "Except me, sometimes." He turned his back on me to rummage in the nearest box. He couldn't know that every time he said the word daughter my heart stuttered, and my belly churned but add on the self-deprecation and the admission of fixing himself of his addictions, and I was a mess for how I should be reacting.

"Joachim—"

"Aha!" He pulled out a pod coffee machine that he immediately plugged in and placed on the small table. "I grabbed some of everything, and I got juice boxes too. Is Soph allowed to have them?"

The way he shortened her name to Soph, it seemed as if it was the most natural thing in the world, making all my thoughts escape.

"Earth to Isaac? Juice?"

"Yeah, good."

He went to his belly on the floor immediately and held out the juice, staying far enough from the cardboard house so he didn't scare her, and then he rested his head on his hands.

"Whatcha doin', Sophie-bug?" he asked and yet another endearment slipped out and took hold of my heart.

"Building a house, but I don't have my bears."

"We'll get them later," I reassured her, but Joachim was already attempting to fix things.

"We'll get you some more bears. What kind of bears do you like?"

"She has bears… they're in her case."

He immediately rolled over, and in one smooth move, he stood and hurried out of the door.

I knew he was going for the bears. With a sigh, I crossed to the coffee machine and rummaged through the pile of pods, finding a caramel coffee, and pushing a mug in place. He was back as fast as I could make the caffeine I desperately needed, arms full of teddies, including Sophie's favorite, B-Bear. Then he was back down on the floor.

"B-Bear!" she exclaimed, and Joachim lifted an eyebrow in question.

"I used the bear as a way of explaining her illness to her and that B was for bear, and so B-Bear stuck," I explained.

"I like it." He gave me an open smile, and it made me weak in the knees.

She took each of her toys into the box, plus a cushion, a juice box, and a bag of chips, and had a tea party to which both Joachim and I were invited. With my caramel latte and his coffee straight-up black, we both lay on our bellies, chatting to Sophie, B-Bear, and all her other bears. She only lasted about thirty minutes. Her eyelids began to droop, and she curled into the cushions, with B-Bear in her arms and her thumb in her mouth, she slipped into sleep.

"Should she do that?" Joachim asked.

"Sleep?"

"No, suck her thumb. I mean I read this article that says it has its place, but I don't know. Should I be giving positive reinforcement to get her to stop, or identifying triggers?"

I never imagined a jock asking a question that had clearly come out of his research.

"She's self-soothing." I turned to him, and we were so close I could see the green flecks around his irises. Too close for comfort. "I want her to have everything that helps her right now," I said. "When she's older…"

I stopped talking, tears choking my throat, which I forced back, and for the longest time, we stared at each other. It was as if there was a bridge between us that was linked in pain. *Fuck this.*

He broke the connection first, blinking and then shifting away from me. "I… I have so much to learn to be a daddy."

"It's a daily thing."

"Will you tell me everything? Was she a good baby?"

I smiled because this was solid ground, and it didn't involve me feeling as if there was a ton of bricks sitting on my chest.

"Loud. When she was born at thirty-six weeks, the doctors were… it was an intense situation, but the moment Sophie was there in the world, she let us know about it."

"Did your sister… did Ashley meet her?"

"For a while." Then I couldn't stop the emotion that choked me, and the first tear tracked down my face.

"Will you tell me?" He reached out to catch the tear, and the compassion in his eyes spoke to me in a hundred different ways. I'd told the story a few times, to specialists, but never to someone with an emotional investment. I didn't have a family. I had one or two friends. No one cared as much as he would. I decided to state the facts without emotion, but that lasted until the first breath.

"She had pre-eclampsia. We thought we'd dealt with the real fear when they delivered Sophie early by cesarean. Only about half an hour in, Ashley's heart stopped. Just like that... one moment she was there—she got to hold Sophie—the next, she was gone."

"And you've cared for Sophie since then?"

"Every day."

Joachim cradled my face, and I held my breath.

"I can never thank you enough, Isaac," he murmured.

"I'm her uncle." *Her daddy. Her everything. Until Joachim.*

He dropped his hand after a moment and then turned to rest his head on his hands again.

"And now she has her daddy too."

Chapter Eight

Joachim

SOMETHING CHANGED IN THE WAY I LOOKED AT ISAAC.

Ever since the day he and Sophie had moved in and we'd had that moment… well, things were different. It had started when I'd cradled his face. There had been a second when I'd seen something more than sadness in his gaze. That quick glimpse of attraction combined with the sizzle that raced down my arm like an electric current from merely cupping his cheek had—

My face met the glass as someone crashed into me from behind. It hurt, but my pride was injured more than my nose, which had bounced off the plexiglass, and I spun around to glower at Moral.

"Hey, asshole, this is practice," I snapped at the big oaf. He patted my helmet, then skated off sniggering. "Asshole," I muttered, then glanced around to see that my teammates were all gathered behind Renco's net making kissy faces at me. "Assholes," I amended then skated to the smirking group. "You couldn't just call my name?"

"We did, five times, yet there you stood staring down at the hoagie ad. You hungry?" Moral asked, then patted his belly as if the hard abs were a beer gut. "We can hit the coffee shop after the scrimmage."

"Any chance we can save the coffee klatch for after practice? First game of the season is tomorrow night," Xander reminded us as he skated up looking very much the team captain. "Also, just a heads-up, Brady is here and sitting up in the rafters with Sinclair. Don't look."

We all looked.

"Dipshits," Xander mumbled.

We all nodded in agreement to his assessment of us and resumed running special-teams drills for another hour. I managed to keep my thoughts on hockey and not on the first stem cell collection that was scheduled for the day after opening day. A simple matter, the oncologists had informed me. Day patient only. In and out in four hours or so. I'd been getting injections at the hospital and was finally notified that my last results showed enough stem cells in my blood. Which was good because Sophie had been feeling poorly the past few days.

Isaac and I had taken turns comforting her so the other could rest, something that Isaac seemed to have trouble with. It was obvious that the man had never had someone else care for his wellbeing. I felt it was my duty to change that as well as tend to my daughter. Which brought us right back to that fizzy feeling popping in my chest like carbonation in a bottle of soda. They both needed me for different reasons, and I was happy... no *thrilled* to give them all that I possessed. It had been too long since I had a family to worry over.

I passed on going to the coffee shop and went right home. It was a glorious fall day in Boston. The air was cool, the sun bright, and the sky as blue as Isaac's eyes. I'd planned a walk to Wigwam Pond on my way home to gather leaves that were dropping. Perhaps we could make a scrapbook or press them somehow. Did people only do that with flowers? I'd have to Google that, but for now a walk to the pond with my two most favorite people in the world was on the docket.

Dropping my personals bag inside the front door, I took a moment to admire my newly-painted living room ceiling, then went in search of Sophie and Isaac. I suspected I knew where to find them. The playhouse.

The door was open to let in that fresh, cool autumn air, but it was quiet inside. Slipping in, I saw both Sophie and Isaac snoozing. She was sprawled out on the floor on a yellow sleeping bag with little red ladybugs, her thumb in her mouth, her long lashes resting on her flushed cheeks. She had dark circles under her eyes, as did Isaac and I. The chemotherapy that she'd had to undergo before the transplant procedure had really done her in, the poor little angel. Again, the knowledge that we were incredibly close to her possibly being cured or in remission filled my heart with hope. It would take time and lots of medical supervision, but we were praying for the best possible outcome. I'd accept nothing less. This had to work. It simply had to…

I sat down beside Isaac, after laying the back of my hand against Sophie's brow. It was warm, but fevers were common I'd quickly learned. My thigh rested against Isaac's, and I let my head drop to the well-padded back of the new sofa. It too was yellow. Sophie liked yellow. And ladybugs. And frogs. Which was why, if she were well enough, I wanted to take her to Wigwam Pond so she could ribbit back to the frogs.

Eyes heavy from being up with a sick child for the past few nights, sleep crept up on me with speed. One moment I'd been mulling over frogs and the next I was out cold. The pressure of someone leaning on me pulled me from my slumber. Shaking off the fuzziness of sleep, I glanced down to see Isaac had curled into my side, his cheek resting on my shoulder, his breath fanning over my chest. My gaze lingered on him, on his lashes and the whiskers that he'd not shaved off this morning. Who had the time or the energy to shave? My face was covered with a reddish-gold beard as well. My back was cramping so I shifted downward a bit, disturbing Isaac with my movement.

His eyes flickered open. I smiled down at him. He smiled weakly back at me. His lips were parted and a mere inch or two from mine. Something profound passed between us as we stared at each other. Perhaps, in hindsight, this would be a mistake of epic proportions or the best thing I'd ever done. Time would tell. I prayed it would not be a mistake. I inhaled his scent and let the lure of those soft pink lips lead me. I lowered my head just a bit. He lifted his chin. Our lips met briefly. Just a mere touch, but it was enough. More than enough. All that fuzzy warm sleepiness was swept aside by something much more primal. It had been some time since I'd been with a man. Women were just easier to hook up with on the road. No one thought much of seeing a player disappear with a sexy chick. Now if that player should slink off with a hot man...

Things were changing, but not so much that same-sex couples didn't raise eyebrows among the fans. Hell, among some of the players as well.

Isaac craned his head, and I applied more pressure. His breath hitched when our tongues touched. A soft moan rolled out of me as his taste blossomed on my taste buds.

"Me make kisses too," Sophie said as she climbed up over us, plunking her bottom to my thigh then plastering both of our faces with sticky little kisses. Isaac blushed furiously, his embarrassment making his brow as warm as Sophie's. Happy and content in a way I never knew I could be I hugged them both to me. My daughter cuddled in tight. Isaac eased out of the familial embrace, his eyes filled with confusion and desire.

"It must be time for lunch," he said as he got to his feet, leaving Sophie in my arms. "I'll go make soup. How does that sound?"

"Mate-o with baby crackers," Sophie requested as she rested on my chest.

"I love tomato soup with tiny crackers too," I told her and got a wobbly smile.

"Daddy like mate-o zoop too," she informed me. My gaze lifted from my daughter to her uncle. I thought that perhaps it was time to start correcting her. *I* was her father. Isaac was not, nor would he ever be. While I understood why she called him that, it was an easier word for a small child to say, she was not his daughter. She was mine. I'd already contacted my lawyer to begin the legal process of setting up my parental rights. As soon as I heard back from him and we had this medical procedure behind us, I'd announce the good news to Isaac and then the world. He'd then be free to live his life as he wished.

Hopefully, given the heat and impact of that kiss, he'd stay here in Boston. He could find a good job in such a big city, get his own place, and live the life of a young, single man without the responsibility of taking care of a child. That was my role now, and I looked forward to Sophie being in my life.

"Let me go open two cans then," Isaac said, then rushed to the house as if someone had bitten him on the backside.

"Wook at clouds." Sophie slithered from my arms to lie on the sofa so she could stare through the glass ceiling. I sat beside her, marveling at how tiny her feet were as they rested on my thigh. Perfect little feet with perfect little toes. "See da clouds! Ooooo fuffy."

I let my head fall back, and we watched clouds floating by until Isaac texted me to let me know lunch was on the table. With Sophie riding on my hip, we went inside. Isaac glanced at me as I handed my girl over so she could wash her hands at the kitchen sink. I saw so many warring emotions that I wasn't sure which to deal with first or if I should deal with it at all. Maybe he needed time to come to grips with this new dynamic. He seemed the sort that required long periods of introspection before he could accept new things, whereas I tended to crash into things full speed then reflect on the aftereffects of the impact later. Which explained why I'd nearly tanked my career.

"We'll talk tonight after my meeting," I told Isaac and that helped to wash away the deep furrows of worry on his brow. "I regret nothing," I added, and he blinked in surprise.

"Me either," he whispered as he settled Sophie on his hip then carried her to the sink.

"So that chip kind of matches your eyes."

I looked up from the pink medallion in my hand to find Victor smirking at me over coffee and pie. Blueberry pie, and it was quite tasty.

"It's pink," I pointed out.

"I know. Just thought I'd say something to yank you out of the fog you've been in all night. You itchy for a drink or something?" He stabbed his pie with his fork, breaking off a large slab, then spearing it.

"No, no, I'm good. Steady." The coffee shop was what people would coin as "Classic Fifties Diner Chic" on Pinterest. Not that I spent much time on Pinterest. The diner was filled with old people and members of the Boston fire and police departments. We'd taken to coming here after meetings just to talk about things. Life, hockey, our addictions, hockey, kids, hockey. We talked a lot of hockey. Vic knew the sport about as well as anyone, and he was the only recovering puck pusher that I knew here. "I've just got a lot on my mind. The stem cell transfer will be done in less than forty-eight hours."

"That's good though, right?" he asked around his mouthful of pie.

"Yes, very good."

"But you're nervous." I nodded. He swallowed then

washed his bite down with some dark roast coffee. "That's to be expected. When Jackie was fourteen his appendix went schizoid. We rushed him to the hospital and the whole time we were there I thought I was going to fucking die of anxiety. Seriously, the only thing that kept me sober was knowing that my boy needed me clean when he came out of surgery. Well, that and I had Dan to cling to."

"Did your children get sick often?" I enquired as I poked at the flaky crust of my pie with my fork. Vic laughed. My gaze lifted from the slice of pie. "That's funny?"

"Jokey, you have no idea. Kids are always sick or hurt. My daughter plays hockey. She's broken an ankle, two fingers, and had a tooth knocked out. Jackie... well, he's not as athletic as BJ, but he had his share of shit, being beat-up for being genderqueer, bullied, and then the usual kid sicknesses. If you're thinking that once your baby girl is all cured of her cancer—and she will be because Vic K. said so—that she'll never be sick, then you need to clear that thinking out of your brainpan right now."

I blew out a breath. "I'm not sure I can handle her getting hurt. It's been..." I paused to find the right word. "It's been so hard to sit there and watch her suffer. The chemo makes her so sick, and I think her hair is getting thinner. I just..."

He reached over the table to grab my hand. "Hey, you got this. Trust me. You feel shaky at any time you got my number. You call, and I'll be there. You got family, yeah?"

"Just the team."

"Ah, okay, well don't be shy about reaching out to them or the team counselor." He gave my wrist a squeeze.

"There's also her uncle. You and he seem to be close, and by close, I mean *close*."

I made a face that pulled a snort of amusement from my pie-eating companion.

"Yes, Isaac is a fine man. But he has carried the burden of her illness for so long. I want to ease that strain from his back however I can."

"He sounds like a real angel."

"That's gracious of you."

"Gracious, that's my middle name," Vic tossed out amicably, then his expression shifted from joking to serious. "Look, I hate to be the one to bust your bubble here, but dating when you're working the program can cause a person—and I don't mean that person is you, Jokey—but some people have been known to replace their substance abuse problems with a brand-new addiction."

"You mean to relationships or intimacy?"

He nodded. Part of me wished that Victor would go back to being that sarcastic asshole everyone pegged him as being. This serious side of the man was making me nervous.

"Just saying that if you form a strong attachment to that sexy baby uncle that it might be a new addictive behavior, right? You may never learn to stand on your own two feet. Again, not saying that will happen to you, just throwing this out as my role as sponsor extraordinaire." He took another bite of his pie and chewed.

I blinked at him. I had known that he'd worked through his own steps in his own way. Victor didn't seem the sort who stuck to rules and protocol *too* strictly. As if he were one of those magical ones who could just grab hold of their addiction and shove it out the window. While he was a rule breaker, he did have demons of his own.

"Yes, I know all of that," I confessed with a sigh. My brain—perhaps my own demon—was telling me that a new, less harmful addiction might be just what I needed. "Perhaps I need to become addicted to being a father."

He pulled a face as if he'd found a sour berry in his pie.

"Well, see, the thing is that booze was such an important thing in your life that when it's gone it feels as if you've lost your identity." His hazel gaze met and held mine. That made so much sense that it literally stole my breath for a moment.

"It shouldn't have been my whole identity. I had hockey."

He chuckled venomously. "Ah yeah, hockey, that beautiful sexy mistress. She can chew you up and spit you out. Wow, that sounded real Hall and Oates, huh? Point is that it takes a strong man to keep his head on straight while recovering. Let me tell you, I put Dan through some shit when I was coming to grips with my drinking. Just be aware of the pitfalls and don't swap out one addiction for another. That's all I wanted to say in my sponsor voice. Do with it what you will." And just like that he was back to the snarky bastard that I had come to know rather well in such a short time. "Have you fucked him yet?" he asked with a leer, and I gaped. "Enquiring minds want to know."

"Of course not. My daughter is battling cancer. Who can think of sex at such a time?"

"A little comfort goes a long way when you're facing something that difficult. Just saying," he added when I began to grumble in earnest. "You know what Rick Springfield says about human touch."

"I touch him plenty." A red eyebrow flew up his brow. "Not that way. Kindly, softly, a kiss—"

"A kiss?" Damn it. "Tongue kiss?"

"Can we talk about hockey now?"

"Coward," he sniggered, but let the topic drop and launched into a long story about his days in Cayuga, which was the feeder team for Boston. Hockey was safer. Much, much safer.

When the coffee and pie were gone, I thanked Vic and headed home. When I stepped inside, Isaac was sitting on the sofa with his iPad open next to him, watching an old movie, and sipping on something heavy with cinnamon, which I could smell from the door. His gaze moved to me as I toed off my sneakers.

"How was the meeting?" he asked as I sat down beside him, twisting to the side so I could look right at him. He was watching an old movie with James Cagney.

"Good." I showed him my newest chip. He gave me a wide smile. "The pie and coffee were good as well."

"You found a worthy sponsor by the sounds."

"He's a pill at times, but yes he's easy to talk to. He gets me and the hockey world." I studied his face as he nodded. "I'd like to talk with *you* now, if you're up to it?" Sophie was asleep in her newly-painted room I was sure or the iPad wouldn't be playing an old gangster flick. "I think we have things we need to discuss."

"The kiss."

I nodded. The kiss.

How could a small touch of lips change so much?

Chapter Nine

Isaac

I understood that we needed to clear the air, but I'd hoped that it would be at some nebulous time in the future. Like *way* in the future when I had my head straight and wasn't running on empty. It's impossible for me to deny that the way he'd touched my face, cradled me, and kissed me had sent shivers down my spine and not just because it turned me on to the point I could have climbed him like a tree. The feeling I had was one of longing, of companionship, of sharing this awful time with someone who had a real stake in the outcome. The specialists, the doctors, the nurses, they all cared, but none of them had connected to my fears the way Joachim had. It was as if his simple touch alone was enough to still the terrors buzzing in my head.

"First though, can I just check in on Sophie, if that's okay?"

He was waiting for my permission. Half of me wanted

to wave that off because he was her father, the other half was madly protective and wanted him to get my go-ahead.

"Sure, she's only been down about an hour though."

"I'll be really quiet," he said with a smile and proceeded to step back awkwardly and knock into a small table, causing a sippy cup to fall off with a clatter. He glanced at me and there was a smile twitching. "I'll be really quiet from now on."

I wanted to smile back, but a flash of concern over him not being steady on his feet morphed into him having had a drink, which began to spiral into fear. He shouldn't be drinking. He picked up a teddy, not B-Bear—since it was safely in the crib with Sophie—but another one that had an eye patch and came complete with a stuffed parrot.

"Watch the mighty D-Man as he's felled by a teddy bear," he announced as if he was commentating a game, then tossed the teddy onto the far chair where it landed on its furry butt and began to sing the *Pirates of the Caribbean* theme. I leaped for it at the same time as he did, both of us fumbling for the off switch, way too close to each other for comfort. He chuckled, and we both held our breaths to see if we'd woken up Sophie.

Nothing. Silence.

He made an exaggerated tiptoeing action to the hallway then showed me a rueful smile.

No man should make me want things as he did.

I checked the upload of tonight's comic strip. It was at fifty percent and was a continuation of the man in the hotel who saw through the shiny surfaces to social injustices and had one hell of a lot of sex. It was kind of dark for me, considering it had started with my character thinking he was a superhero, but it had gone down well with my subscribers so far, most of whom appreciated it when my guys ended up having sex in the weirdest of places.

Tonight's episode, which would go out in a couple of days, had my hero on his knees in a meat locker with a waiter. I'd pulled no punches in the message that the guest thought he'd earned respect because he was in the penthouse. Social justice warrior for the win. Right now, it was my diehard fans who followed me that were paying the bills back home. Apart from the hospital account, which was something else I needed to talk to Joachim about. Funny how discussing something I didn't want— getting a loan from him—was a more palatable subject than talking about a kiss.

"She's asleep," he stated as he sat next to me on the sofa and glanced at the screen. He wouldn't see much given the angle and the fact the upload screen hid most of it, but I wasn't going to share my work right now. "Have you been working?"

"Fitting it in when I can."

"Can I see some of your work?"

"This is just contract work, it's not my creative art," I lied.

"Can I see some of your creative work then?"

I paused, but he was so wide-eyed and interested, and hell, it meant I didn't have to talk about the kiss. I minimized the upload, then scrolled to another folder and opened some preliminary sketches I'd done of Sophie, holding it up so he could see.

"Holy shit," he muttered and leaned in to examine the sketch. "That's Sophie right there."

"Uh-huh."

"You're so talented."

"Thank you." I resisted the urge to be self-deprecating and tell him that I didn't think I was talented. I had to believe I was because how else was I going to save a college fund for Sophie, or help her buy her first car or…

"Seriously, wow, can I get a copy of that? I mean, buy it, you don't have to give it to me for free." He looked so earnest, but I turned the screen to me, and in a few strokes, I'd sent it to his phone, hearing the ping as it hit his inbox. He opened his phone immediately and spent a good minute zooming in and examining it closely.

"Am I able to get it printed? Is this in pencil? Would you do another one for the wall in color?"

"It's mostly just for me."

"I'd love to have a picture of my daughter done by the other man in her life." He smiled at me.

"I just need to see her well before I can…"

He sobered immediately. "I know." He closed his phone and put it on the side table, tapping it a couple of times. "How was she today?"

That was a loaded question. Fractious, scared, exhausted, happy, playing, not playing, it was a roller coaster of actions and responses that drained her until she'd fallen asleep about an hour ago.

"As well as expected," I kept my tone upbeat.

"Day after tomorrow…" He didn't have to elaborate. On Thursday, the hospital was harvesting what they needed, and then it was a waiting game, but at least I had hope now.

"Yeah."

"So, we need to talk."

I paused, then turned off the iPad, wanting every piece of concentration I had left to work together to handle this conversation.

"Okay." I imagined the letdown now, the words that Joachim would use to explain how the kiss was okay, but that he wasn't interested.

"I haven't had sex in over a year," he blurted and went scarlet.

I fumbled for a reply because that was some statement. "Me neither," I admitted after a pause. "Two for me. Not since…" *Before my sister died.*

"When I kissed you, it felt like…"

"It felt good," I finished for him.

"Yeah, and it wasn't just a craving for sex, it was a connection. I want to do it again…"

I hesitated to answer because I sensed a *but* after that statement. "But?"

He closed his eyes briefly. "I'm not a stupid man. I'll always be an addict. My sponsor said some things tonight that I already knew. About dating when I was working the program, and how I could end up replacing the abuse with another addiction."

"An addiction to what?"

His gaze dipped to my lips then back to my eyes. "To your lips, to you as a concept, to your body, to the love you give my daughter, to sex."

Was he really calling me an addiction? That was a huge jump from one kiss to suggesting I was bad for him. I didn't know how I should feel right now. Pleased that our gentle kiss had rocked his world or pissed that what happened needed to be analyzed to death. I had my own demons to fight, and I didn't want—or need—to be drawn into someone else's drama.

"It's best we don't do it again. You should focus on yourself," I murmured, acute disappointment and relief fighting for dominance. I didn't want to start my own addiction to imagining me with Joachim and Sophie as this small family with a happy ever after because sure as eggs were eggs that is exactly where my brain would go. One kiss didn't mean forever, but Joachim was dangerous to my libido, and when I added Sophie to the mix, it was just a recipe for heartbreak.

"I know it's for my own good," he said after the longest pause. "I listened to what my sponsor said, and I've read the same things. I understand them on an intellectual level, but at the same time, knowing it could impact my recovery, plus finding out I'm a dad, plus everything Sophie is dealing with…"

"What?"

Anguished, he scrubbed at his eyes, then twisted one hand in his hair. "All I want to do is kiss you again."

"But it's not a good idea," I said because I knew he needed to hear that from me. I didn't know him very well, but I'd seen him with Sophie, and I knew he was a kind man who cared. He deserved my compassion and support for that alone.

I stood and stretched, picked up my iPad and mug, and headed for the kitchen with Joachim close behind.

"I'm sorry," he said as I rinsed the mug and placed it in the dishwasher. "Just when I find Sophie and the something with you… shit, I'm making things awkward aren't I."

I schooled my expression before I turned to face him. He was leaning against the door jamb, six feet between us, and he looked so pathetically sad and beaten, and my caring side kicked up a notch, so much that I wanted to pull him into a hug and tell him it was okay.

It wasn't okay. He was in pain. Sophie was in pain. And I was the only one who could handle everything that could be thrown at us now.

"No, you haven't made anything awkward." I wasn't going to leave the kitchen until he moved though, and maybe that was a little uncomfortable. Not to mention the insane pull to hug him and kiss him again.

"Hashtag fucked up timing," he muttered and then moved out of the way to let me pass. With my iPad close to my chest, I kept my head down and focused on getting out of the kitchen without doing something stupid. He tugged my shirt as I passed, and I spun on a dime, his face *right there*, and with it was the internal argument playing out in his expression in real time. Regret, want, decisions, it was all plain to see. "I'm sorry," he said brokenly.

"It's not just you. I don't want to lose sight of what we're doing here for Sophie. I picture a day when we're back home, and she's well, and that's all that matters."

He opened his mouth to speak, then appeared to stop himself and released his hold on my shirt.

"That's all that matters," he repeated. "Sophie."

I nodded and went into her room, sitting on the bed next to her crib. Joachim had offered me a separate room, but this was where I wanted to be. From here I could reach out and touch her, reassure myself she was breathing, that she wasn't too hot or cold or needed me in any way. My iPad vibrated to indicate the upload had finished, and I double-checked it was all in place and ready to go live in two days.

By then Sophie would have received the stem cells, and she'd be in the hospital for maybe six or eight weeks. The first step in her recovery would be done, and we'd be following the path to her being well.

Because she *was* going to recover from this. Joachim's stem cells would replenish what the chemo was destroying in her bone marrow, and she would live to go to school, prom, graduation, college. She'd meet someone, or not. I didn't care what she did if she was happy.

With all my thoughts in order I laid back on the bed.

But it took me a long time to fall asleep.

"How are you feeling?"

D-Day had arrived without fanfare. The doctors said that Joachim's levels were ready so they could take blood. Sophie and I sat with him as they put a cannula into a vein in each arm and watched the blood pass through tubes that connected to the cell separator where the stem cells were collected. We weren't sure whether it would be enough today, but the specialist seemed happy enough at the progress so far. I held hope that this was all they required and that in two days they could inject Sophie with what she needed. She was hot today, listless. She clung to me and slept on my chest, and I wanted to reach out and hold Joachim's hand, to thank him for what he was doing, but also to connect the three of us who were fighting this battle.

I didn't... because it was too much.

"Hey." I heard a voice and glanced over at the door where someone was standing in a Boston Rebels hockey shirt. The last thing we needed in here were fans who wanted an autograph. I stiffened, ready to tell whoever it was to fuck off, but then I recognized him. Xander, captain of the Rebels.

"Hey, Cap." Joachim smiled up at him.

"Okay to come in?"

Joachim glanced at me. "Sure." Xander sidled in, followed by a younger guy. Each of them stood respectfully by the wall and didn't come closer.

"Wanted to check in on you," Xander said. "How're you all doing?"

"Good. Isaac, this is my captain, Xander, and Austin from the team."

Austin sketched a wave, and Xander nodded.

"It's good to meet you," Xander offered. "If there's anything the team can do to help your niece, you just have to ask."

Niece. I both hated and loved that word at the same time. It gave me a link to Sophie that would never be broken, but at the same time it pushed me aside.

Ignore this feeling. Sophie is the important one.

"Thank you," I said with feeling. Sophie stirred in my arms, and I smoothed a hand over her thinning curls, cradling her head and wishing it was two days already so she could start getting better. Xander elbowed Austin, who blushed bright red.

"Uhm, we brought some stuff for Sophie." Austin placed a bag on the ground. "Some of the tiniest shirts I've ever seen, and this hockey game that… for when she's better." Austin's eyes were bright with emotion.

"Thank you, she'll love it."

"And a shirt for you," Austin added. "I'm sorry Sophie is so ill."

So am I. "Thank you."

"Did you watch the tape I sent you," Joachim asked.

"I did," Xander murmured, leaning back against the wall. "Chicago put up a good fight against…"

The world of hockey spun around me. I knew Joachim was going to miss at least one game because of what he was doing, but since a donor recovery could be anywhere from two days to three weeks, it could be longer. Tomorrow's game was against New York, and I'd heard him on the phone this morning talking defense strategies that I had no idea about. There was a blue line, there was this cross, and that defense, and he spoke about it all so passionately—as fervently as he talked about making a life for Sophie when she was well. I stared out the window at the view beyond, the city not that far and the sky a bright blue, and wondered if my heart would survive this future he was so excited about.

And what my place would be in it.

Chapter Ten

Joachim

THE NEXT TWO WEEKS SPED BY IN A BLUR OF HOPE AND hockey. Lots of things changed in small ways, like Isaac and I growing closer, talking for hours, watching stupid Netflix shows, and holding hands like kids. He knew how I liked my coffee, I knew he hated anchovies on pizza, he understood my pre-game superstitions, I knew all about his cartoons and how good he was at art.

I was falling for him, and it scared me.

The biggest change in our lives was that Sophie had come through the transplant procedure really well, but was now in isolation for at least six to eight weeks. The staff at the hospital were top-notch and incredibly well-trained, but still, that was a long time for a small child to be confined to a small room. And while I understood the reasoning—she was incredibly susceptible to infections at this stage of her treatment—I longed to take her and Isaac home and go skip rocks across Wigwam Pond.

Isaac was carrying more than his share of the burden as I had hockey to play. I'd missed a week, or three games, due to the team physician being overly cautious about the procedure to harvest the blood. Better safe than sorry he had said. I'd felt fine, but I'd been overruled. So, while I sat around with my thumb up my ass, Nick had inundated me with press and social media nonsense.

"The whole hockey world wants to be kept in the loop," the Rebels owner had said a few hundred times. He desperately wanted the PR team to have access to Sophie, but that was a no-go and no way, so I sent out updates minus any images. Only Isaac and I were allowed in, and even that made me nervous as I was exposed to *so* many people. A whole plane filled with men who had children and significant others. God only knows what kind of germs the Rebels had.

I was extra diligent about trying to sanitize myself before seeing my daughter. Isaac teased that I bathed in hand sanitizer, but that wasn't far from the truth. Hell, if I had to gargle with alcohol and/or flush my bowels with bleach, I'd do it. It would suck, but I'd do it. Perhaps I had already swapped out my drinking addiction for the fatherhood one. If so, then that was just how it would be. Nothing was more important than Sophie and Isaac. Not even hockey. And that sexy siren had been my lone companion for many a year. Amazing how one small poppet of a child could turn your whole world upside down.

I was also addicted to friendship. Not just the way the team embraced me, but the way Isaac talked to me about everything and nothing, and made me smile on a daily basis. I liked being his friend, I liked having a friend, but every small kiss I stole was another tick in the list that meant what we had was more than friendship.

I glanced from my phone and the latest text from Isaac as the rest of the team readied themselves for a game against Harrisburg. The new season had just started, and we were still kind of feeling each other out in terms of lines and defensive pairings. The press had been salivating over the fact that we'd just signed Brady Rowe as our new defensive coach, a move that had thrilled everyone in Boston from the oldest to the youngest Rebels fan. It also meant that he'd be playing a chess game with his brother-in-law, Jared Madsen, who was the Railers defensive coach.

Brady had pulled all the D-men to the side in our hotel just two hours ago, his smile wide, his tie just a little askew, which was typical retired D-man for sure. He'd given us a short pep talk and vowed to do his best to ensure our defense was top-notch, but he needed our cooperation to do so. Then he'd paired me with Xander Holden. Just. Like. That. I was still taken aback at the notion. I was a new man on the team, wobbly as a colt in terms of my addiction, and here the coach had given me Xander to play with. Even now with the decision announced and the game roster set, I still felt as if a mistake had been made. But I had to trust Brady's knowledge of the game, the opposition, and our team.

I texted Isaac as the team chatted and readied themselves for the game.

J—Will u watch the game with Sophie?

I—**We've got the pregame show on now. Go make good hockey!**

    J-I miss you guys xx

    I-We miss you too x

Isaac sent an image of himself and Sophie—both in Rebels jerseys—her propped up with pillows and him curled up next to her. She looked wan and tired. Her beautiful hair had mostly fallen out now, so we'd taken to tying bright scarves around her head. She got to pick them out. That had also gotten a mention in one of my updates, and the Rebels main office had been inundated with specially made cancer chemo caps for children in beautiful fun patterns and colors.

Sophie had hundreds of scarves and chemo caps to pick from, and we'd donated a ton of them to the hospital here and posted a message on the team's social media to thank everyone who'd sent them in. Tonight, Sophie was wearing one that was gold and black to match her tiny jersey, the one with my number, but the word DADDY across the back where my last name would normally be.

I smiled at the reminder of the little jersey. Smiling was becoming very common. Despite Isaac and me being exhausted mentally and physically, we were feeling hopeful. Wary, but hopeful. Sophie wasn't eating well, she was nauseated with some diarrhea, which was, we had been assured many times, a normal reaction. Even though she was having to deal with those problems, her test results were encouraging, which was one of the reasons for the smiling. There was still so much for us to get through, but we'd get there, one step at a time. Together.

"You ready?"

I glanced up at Xander's voice. The rest of the team were lined up, bumping fists, or rubbing heads as players did before a game. Moral had this thing that he had to slam his considerable chest into the chest of each Rebel as we came into the tunnel.

"Yeah. I'm ready." I showed him the image. He smiled warmly. "Pretty, huh?"

"Which one?" I blinked. Xander chucked my shoulder. "Yes, she's pretty. Isaac isn't too hard on the eyes either." I must have looked at him oddly because the playful smile fell from his handsome face. "I was kidding. I mean he's adorable, but I'm not saying that I've noticed that he was cute. I mean I did notice, but I'm happily committed."

"Yes, of course, I know you're happy with Mason." I pushed to my skates as concern swept through me. "If I gave you a thought that I was…" I fished around for the word.

"Jealous?" His eyes twinkled now with mirth. "It's fine. We're all pretty aware of how you're beginning to feel about Isaac."

He lumbered off. I stared at his back as he exited the away locker room, my jaw hanging open. *Jealous.*

"I'm not jealous," I mumbled, tossed my phone into my personals bag, and then followed my new defensive partner out to the tunnel.

The boys were loud, pumped up to be playing the Railers, and their energy was contagious. Moral thundered over to me; his red beard now braided into a plait as if he were a dwarf from Middle Earth. There was nothing small about his chest bump though. It nearly sent me through a wall. He laughed when I stumbled, then rubbed my face with a stinky glove. Normally that would be an insult, but with Moral, it was a sign of affection since he did it to everyone after he knocked them through the wall.

After the Railers were introduced to thunderous applause from the Harrisburg fans, we hit the ice. Boos rained down on us. I hardly heard the noise from the fans filling the packed arena. My mind was back on the jealous comment as we made a few laps on the ice, then took our places for the national anthem. I was on the starting line, so I stood there next to Xander, our captain, with my head down as a chubby man in a Railers sweater sang loud and strong.

Jealous. That's silly. There's no jealousy. Isaac and I had set aside any attraction that we'd been feeling to devote one-hundred-percent of our attention to Sophie. How could I be jealous of something that wasn't there? Or had the feelings that had started to blossom merely been shoved into the dark like a tender flower bulb emerging too soon for its own good, so the florist tucks it into a closet to stall its growth?

"… and the home of the brave." I snapped back to the song and the present as the fans clapped at the end of the anthem. We made our way to our positions. I gave Adler Lockhart a wide grin as he nestled into my side for the opening faceoff.

"Bet you're too full of chowder to keep up with me," the mouthy ass chirped.

"No worries. I ate Boston baked beans for lunch, so I'll have plenty of gas," I parried and got a snort of amusement from the Railers number one mouth. Looked like I'd be squaring up with him for the time being, which was fine. I'd played against the Railers more than once and knew my job well. My gaze moved from Adler making noise about farts to the showdown over the puck. Marquis squared off against Tennant Rowe. The official gave both men a warning about encroachment before dropping the puck. Lockhart drove an elbow into my side as Rowe cleanly won the faceoff. Tennant had been the league leader in faceoff wins for years now, and it was evident as to why… he was mad fast. But Marquis was no slouch and was at my side in a flash as the puck hit Adler's stick. I knocked Lockhart to his ass, stole the puck, and pushed it to Marquis.

"Beans the musical fruit," I shouted down at Adler, then raced off to the Railers end to help keep the lanes open for a shot attempt. Marquis snapped it high, but Stan Lyamin was ready for the snapshot and caught it with ease. The puck was tossed to a linesman and with that nice attempt the game began in earnest.

We played a tight two periods despite not being familiar with my defensive partner. Xander was a talkative player who wasn't afraid to take anyone to the boards, which was my style as well. Hockey pundits liked to say I "played on the edge" or that I "played with grit," which was just a nice way to say "I liked to fight." Which wasn't true. Mostly. I did not go out of my way to get into a fight, but when a fight was needed, then I didn't back away. Calling us goons or instigators wasn't acceptable in this new era of hockey, but I knew my job. I liked to think of myself as Wolverine in an older comic that I had read on a long flight home a few years ago. Sue me, I enjoyed a comic book on occasion. The point being that Iron Man and Captain America knew that on occasion they would need someone who was willing to get bloody aka kill someone. Since neither of them, nor the rest of the Avengers, ever crossed that line, they brought in a feral, short Canuck to do the dirty work when it was needed. That was me, but I wasn't short or Canadian, although I *could* turn feral if need be, to protect the elite players from sullying themselves.

Our elite players were Austin, Marquis, and our goalie, Renco. I watched out for them, just as Adler protected Tennant and Stan the Mighty Russian in their crease. So, it stood to reason that when Lockhart took a poke at Renco in the third period of a zero-zero game, I took a little offense and gave him a shove that sent him tumbling over Dieter Lehmann. Moral showed up, then spouted off as he did. Someone's mother loving goats was mentioned by the big man with the beard braid, and Adler threw a fist. Knowing we needed something to get our offense going, I grabbed Lockhart by the head, popped off his skid lid, and hit him in the face. To which he replied with an upper cut that landed soundly on my jaw. We fell to the ice pulling on each other's jerseys as whistles blew.

When we got to our skates the fans were applauding and yelling.

"Good one, J-Man," Adler said as we skated to our respective boxes for our bad boy timeouts.

"Nice upper cut," I shouted back before I entered the sin bin and took my seat. My jaw would ache for a bit, but the team was pretty fired up now, so mission successful.

We went on to win the game in overtime with a quirky

little shot from Austin that bounced off Erik Gunnarsson's skate, then slid between Stan's legs before he could close off his five hole. It was a sound win against an incredibly tough team. Brady was ecstatic afterward and gave every D-man a Hershey kiss. I popped the tiny little chocolate treat into my mouth as I made my way into the dressing room for all the post-game nonsense.

I made sure I was polite and humble, as that was hockey player etiquette, but I was in a hurry to wrap this up so I could check on Sophie and Isaac. It seemed to take forever, but the press finally cleared out and I dove on my phone like a man possessed. And I *was* possessed—with worry. Something might have gone drastically wrong during the game. Yes, Isaac had the owner's private number, as well as each coach's in case of a dire emergency so that I could be pulled out if need be. And no one had said word one about any kind of setback or emergency call but still…

It came to me as I sat in my sweaty gear with the ripe scent of unwashed man surrounding me that I had truly become a parent. Worry was one thing that every father and mother did even when they had no reason to worry. Sophie had been doing well and would continue to improve. There could be no other outcome. Still, it wasn't until I was finally able to Facetime with Isaac and see my daughter resting peacefully—she'd conked out before the second period got underway—I could truly breathe again.

"I'll be home tomorrow," I told Isaac. He nodded and rose from the bed that he'd be sleeping in for the next six or so weeks. He looked so tired. I wished I could be there all the time as he was, but my job demanded that I play.

And since it was hockey that was allowing me to pay all the bills that were quickly piling up, I had to be on the ice. Sophie was now on my insurance after a long and nasty battle with the insurance company. They hated pre-existing conditions and were balking at adding her until the public furor over it made them reconsider the situation. Which was a blessing because just covering what the insurance wouldn't was going to drain my bank account quickly. If only I hadn't drunk so much money away...

"I remember. She misses you." He padded away from the bed and into the bathroom so we could speak without disturbing her rest. "She thinks you have rocket skates."

That made me snigger. "It was the beans," I replied, then had to explain the whole conversation with Lockhart to him. He laughed softly, the sound soothing and soft. "I miss you too," I said, and he stared at me with weary eyes. "I mean her. Well, no, I mean I miss you both."

"Same. We really shouldn't be missing each other like that though," he whispered as he closed the bathroom door then leaned against it.

"No, I know but there is no controlling the human heart."

He bit down on his lip, and I was hard in an instant. The man was killing me, but God above it was a sweet death.

"What would your sponsor say?"

"He'd tell me to be careful, then to make mad passionate love to you. Not in those exact words," I whispered, then was hit in the side of the head with a balled-up sock. It was wet and stank. My gaze flew to Austin who was wide-eyed. He pointed to Xander, who whipped his other sock at my face. I ducked and Renco caught the sock with his left hand with ease. A proud smile played on our goalie's face. "This isn't the time or place for this discussion."

"I can see that." Isaac chuckled. "Maybe we could reevaluate things?"

My heart stuttered. "Yes, we could possibly do that. When I get home tomorrow, we can maybe sneak off for dinner? Just us to talk and reevaluate?"

I saw the flash of concern in his gaze. He pondered on that suggestion for some time, then gave me a single nod. If not for the room of sweaty, rowdy, half-naked Rebels I would have hooted in glee. Instead, I gave Isaac my warmest smile, which got me one of his shyest ones.

"Tomorrow then. I'll see you around three or so. Kiss Sophie for me."

"I will. Congrats on the win." He ended the call. I sat there staring at my now dark phone, my gut all tangled up, my smile wide. Tomorrow. We'd talk again tomorrow. There were so many things I wanted to tell him. About me, us, Sophie, the future that I hoped and prayed we would have now that my lawyer had my paperwork ready to submit to the courts. Soon I'd be named Sophie's father legally. Yes, tomorrow couldn't come soon enough.

Chapter Eleven

Isaac

THE CONCEPT OF A FIRST DATE WHEN I ALREADY LIVED with Joachim was weird. Spending time away from Sophie was strange. My whole life was on hold, and I was exhausted with the oddness of it all. I hadn't had a date in over two years, maybe more, hell I can't recall the last time I sat down with another man and talked about music or food or movies.

Before Ashley died for sure.

Three years.

Jesus.

I'd showered. I'd shaved. I even took time to choose the right shirt, which came from my limited supply. We'd decided to walk to a local place, a hole-in-the-wall Italian restaurant that Joachim said he'd heard good things about. I worried it was exposing him to alcohol, and that a restaurant visit would enable him. I was concerned that the hospital might need us. Most of all, I wasn't hungry.

I was tired. Worried about Sophie—scared. The news today had been good, she was improving day to day. They told us that it might only be two more weeks and we could bring her home. That was amazing news, but the home part left me cold. Joachim talked at length about the things he could do with the house, from extending it, to converting rooms, to fitting a new kitchen, all to make sure that Sophie had the best place to live with his budget. I didn't know how much money he had then, but the house was his with no loans or debts, and I knew he was earning a million this year from the team.

A million dollars. For a year's work.

When Sophie's treatment was finished and paid for, he could do anything he wanted to do to the house and have money left over for whatever it was that millionaire hockey players did with their free time normally. Vacations, women, men, luxury, investments, stable futures, it was a long list of awesome things that he could have that would make Sophie's life secure.

Not like me. Self-employed artist, in the place that Ashley and I had bought with our small inheritance, with not a cent to my name.

I glanced at my watch. He said he'd be home at seven, but it was ten minutes past, and he wasn't here yet. I know his meetings sometimes ran late, depending on if he stayed back and chatted with his sponsor, so I wasn't worried, but I was *so* tired. I slumped into one corner of the sofa, trying not to crease my shirt too much because I wanted to make a decent effort at how I looked. I spent a few moments flicking through my phone, catching up on work emails in that halfhearted way that meant I should really leave it alone. When I couldn't spell the word "sincerely" and had mangled it so bad that not even spellcheck had an option, I closed my email, reached over to put my cell on the table, then slid lower into the sofa. I could live with a creased shirt if I could just close my eyes for a few moments, and it wouldn't hurt just to rest.

I really need to stay awake. Why am I walking through the wards looking for Sophie? Where is she? I should be at home. She's fine.

"… hey."

Leave me alone. I need to find Sophie.

"… bed," the person said again. Joachim. He was talking and stroking my hair, and I half woke as he levered me to stand and then lifted me up off my feet and supported me to the bedroom.

Where's Sophie? She's okay. The doctor is telling me everything is okay.

"… sleep… date… kiss."

He kissed me. I smiled into the touch and lifted my hands so I could curl my fingers in his hair, only there was nothing there, and I heard a chuckle.

"… goodnight."

I wriggled my shoes off, or Joachim helped me, I wasn't sure, but he smelled so good, of lemon and spice, and I just wanted another kiss. He pulled the covers over me and my only unwrinkled shirt, and then I closed my eyes again. I couldn't fight the sleep, and I rolled over on my side.

———

SUNSHINE CAST LIGHT ACROSS MY FACE THROUGH A TINY crack in the drapes, and I blinked as I rolled onto my back to escape it. My watch told me it was seven a.m. That was a long ass sleep and one missed date past embarrassing.

"Morning," Joachim said from the door, two mugs in hand, and smiling at me.

"Hey," I croaked and cleared my scratchy throat, counting down from five so I could compose myself. "Sorry," I offered as he placed the coffee next to me and perched on the edge of my bed.

"I checked in with the hospital—"

"What? Is Sophie okay?" I scooted back to sit up with the help of a pile of pillows as panic gripped me.

"She's wonderful, had a good night, slept through apparently, a bit like her uncle Isaac."

"Shit." I calmed my breathing and quelled my instinct to panic at the slightest misspoken word. "I need to wake up."

"Caffeine helps." He nudged the mug a little, and I picked it up, careful not to spill anything on my now creased shirt. The first sip was hot and so damn perfect I could have cried.

"Sorry about last night," I said after the caffeine began to kick in and he made no move to leave the room or his place on my bed.

"Sorry for what? The date? Don't even think about it. We're exhausted, and I went straight to bed after tucking you in and slept until five."

I closed my eyes briefly and then rolled my neck, falling on what was left of my coffee like a man possessed. Only when it was gone and I felt the effect of it, did I focus properly and see Joachim was in a Rebels T-shirt, the eagle on the front a reminder that he was due at the arena for morning practice at nine. I remembered that because we'd said we wouldn't be out late on our date.

"What do you do at work?" I blurted, my gaze traveling from the logo up to his face. "When it's not a game, I mean. Conditioning, I guess? Fight practice? Do you fight with your team? That wouldn't be right because you could hurt… I'm stopping now."

He chuckled at the deluge of questions. "We don't know from one practice to another what the coaches want us to focus on. Unless we have a particular issue that we bring up, then it's coach-led. Yesterday I was working on special teams with Xander."

"The captain and the other half of your defense pairing." I was proud I could remember that and even more so when he nodded.

"I was honing my back check."

"What exactly is a back check."

"I'm skating backward toward our goal and closely defending against the offensive rushes of an opposing player." He wiggled his fingers as if that helped, but just the idea of skating forward at speed was terrifying, let alone backward. He carried on. "We practiced with three forwards on penalty kills, defensive teams, and then attack strategies for when we're one man down."

Okay, none of that was staying in my head right now. I didn't know enough about hockey to understand, although I had heard the term penalty kill in the games I'd watched in Sophie's room. I knew sometimes the guys in the boxes meant one team had less players or was it the other team who had more? I didn't know because mostly I'd been watching Joachim, and dozing, or reading to Sophie, so none of what I watched stuck with me.

"I need to watch more hockey. I will do that when Sophie… when we don't have the hospital visits and…" I sighed.

He took the empty mug from me, placed it carefully next to his, and then in a smooth move, he joined me on the bed, sliding in so he could put his arm around me before tugging me back into his embrace. Someone squeaked.

I think it was me.

"We'll have another date," he said as he wrapped me in a huge bear hug, enough so that all the fearful voices in my head quieted.

"Okay."

"When we're not tired."

"Uh-huh." I turned my face into him, inhaling the spicy lemon, and burying myself in his hold. I could get used to this, and maybe when Sophie and I go back home, he'd want to keep this up, more dates as he got to know Sophie, so maybe one day we could be a small family, all together. I don't know how it would work, with me and Sophie in Florida, and him in Boston, but maybe one of us could move. Me probably because my work was online, nothing kept me down there. I would miss the sunshine… I would miss my home… but one day things might change. I wouldn't be able to visit the graveyard to talk to Ashley or my parents when things happened, but that was something I could come to terms with. I would do anything for Sophie, and maybe I could find a piece of happy too.

I inhaled his scent.

"Are you sniffing me?" He chuckled, and his chest moved under my cheek.

"I can't help it. You smell good," I murmured. "Sorry about falling asleep last night, I was looking forward to the date."

"It's cool. You know, I like this a lot, just lying here hugging."

"Me too."

"Isaac?"

"Hmm?"

"I like you."

"I'm a pretty likable guy," I teased.

"No, I mean, I *like you* like you." Before I could answer, he gave one last squeeze and then extricated himself, pressing a kiss to the top of my head. "I'll see you at the hospital this afternoon."

I returned his smile and slid down into the covers after I heard the front door shut. All I could think was that he *likes me* likes me. I felt like a kid again, waiting for a promise ring, and for a moment, I forgot everything apart from the hope and a bright future that was out there if I was lucky enough with Sophie leukemia-free and my heart healed. Of course, there was the thorny issue that what was blooming between me and Joachim was a culmination of proximity, stress, and exhaustion, which on their own could be reason to seek comfort together. Added together they were the perfect storm for a situation where we shared support.

It wasn't real *like*.

Not really.

We finally made it to the Italian restaurant, Romano's, the night before Sophie was due to come home, and it was a celebration, as well as what I guessed was our first official first date—mostly because we'd made it out of the house. We'd talked about going out on several occasions, but we'd had a series of events that delayed it from happening. I'd fallen asleep on the sofa before two of them, Joachim nursed a strained muscle on another, and sometimes we only got as far as Netflix and popcorn. There'd been the odd kiss here and there, but tonight was the night before a very special day because Sophie's discharge was a go, and the test results were positive.

The goal of Sophie's induction chemotherapy was to achieve remission, and the last results yesterday confirmed there were no leukemia cells in her bone marrow samples. This didn't mean she was cured, but the normal marrow cells had returned, and her blood counts were at expected levels. The more intense consolidation phase of chemo would be next and might last for several months to reduce the number of leukemia cells still in the body. It wasn't going to be an easy road for her, but I had to take the wins when I could.

Tomorrow she was coming home. Tonight, I was going to take an hour to eat Italian food and try to calm my racing thoughts.

The menu was simple. The owners were big boisterous Italians who knew Joachim and were determined to have him taste everything on the menu. I guess this was part and parcel of fame, but I couldn't help but be sucked into their excitement of having Joachim eat at their restaurant. Added to that, Sophie's journey was just starting, but hope burned in my heart, and I was high on positivity. He took a few selfies and signed napkins, but people mostly left us alone. We talked some about hockey, baseball—I was a fan, he wasn't—football, both of us watched at Thanksgiving, and my art. He constantly moved the conversation back to my art, which was flattering, particularly when he showed me the comments in his chat group from some of the players on the team.

"Some of the guys wanted me to ask you if you were interested in commissions, but I wasn't sure if that was what you do."

"I can if they're serious." It might be a good way to get some money back in the account before we left Boston. Sophie needed a ton of stuff, and I couldn't ask Joachim for any more than he was already giving. My new comic strip had grown my audience, something resonating about my millionaire, who was now a billionaire, and the idiot things he was doing with his money. The last one was where he bought a Fabergé egg and then smashed it just because it was fun, had gone viral. Apparently, it had captured the attention of a couple of influencers. They'd reshared it and my subscriptions quadrupled overnight. It wasn't thousands of dollars, but it was a small regular income that would be monthly, if I came up with ideas each day.

"Dunny loves his cars. He said he wants a painting of his Ferrari for his garage. It's his baby."

"The garage?"

"Nah, the car. At least, I think so. The garage holds so much of his collection, who knows."

"Have you seen the Ferrari?"

"God no, he doesn't actually take it out, apparently he just polishes it. A lot." Joachim snorted a laugh. "Take advantage of my idiot team, professional hockey players have money to burn." He winced the moment he realized what he said, then stared down at his empty plate. "Not me, I mean, other hockey players. All I did was fuck myself over."

I took his hand and squeezed, and he glanced up at me, before turning his hand and lacing our fingers.

"Rookie contract, endorsements at the start, less so when the alcohol took hold, but the big money was there. I mean I'm no Tennant Rowe, but I've blown millions. Parties, cars, unwise investments, gambling. I gave away a lot of it in donations, so there was that, but I'm a fucking ridiculous human being."

I heard all the stuff he didn't say, about how his life choices were all skewed by his addiction, and all I felt was compassion. I couldn't understand how someone could become so broken and dependent, and how he'd lost so much, but I could see he regretted it all.

"I have a chance at an endorsement contract with Bauer, nothing amazing, but enough to start building a college fund, if that's what Sophie wants to do. Then there's my next contract, my agent is angling for three years." He paused, and the introspection slipped into melancholy.

"Three years playing in Boston?"

"If I keep my nose clean, head down, do the work, then

I hope so. They're everything I want in a team, not that my old team was bad. I just burned too many bridges with them y'know, letting the team down, the rehabs that never stuck. I'm surprised I lasted as long there as I did, but they were good guys down there."

"So, three years *in* Boston?" I had to be sure what he meant.

"Then I'll retire? Maybe move into coaching, use my sparkling personality to become a pundit." He snorted a laugh then, and it made me smile. He could so host some show where he talked hockey, I could see it now, probably all dressed up in a suit and wielding stats like an expert.

"You'll be able to do anything you put your mind to," I murmured, although the idea of three years in Boston meant that if anything came of me and him, then Sophie and I would need to uproot from Florida.

"I want to be a good dad. Do you think I can be that?" There was desperation in his voice, and I couldn't believe he was looking for me to reassure him. We'd known each other eight weeks or so, but I'd seen a lot in that short time. The way he cradled Sophie, the way he cried for her, the times he'd held me and supported me, I think that he had a huge well of compassion and love that would make him a very good dad.

"I haven't known you long," I cautioned. "But you've accepted your role in Sophie's life with determination, and I see the hard work you're putting into your sobriety and your team. You'll be a good dad." He seemed grateful for the words, but his gaze slipped to the table next to us, and he winced.

They were celebrating a birthday, with champagne and

cake and singing, and even though we'd deliberately chosen a table far from the bar and requested soda with our meal, there were reminders of alcohol everywhere.

"I'm tired," I lied. "You want to get out of here?" He looked so relieved that I wished I'd thought of it before. We didn't have to come to a restaurant for a date, we could have sat by the pond and stared at the stars, and I would have felt just as happy.

"Yeah. I'm tired too," he lied back to me.

He cleared the check, and before too long we were out on the sidewalk. He immediately relaxed, then hand in hand we were heading for Wigwam Pond and his home. When we got inside, he paused in the hall and reached for my hand.

"I really do like you," he murmured, and my heart filled with a rare happiness. Sophie was coming home, and I was attracted to Joachim.

I carded my fingers into his hair, knowing that he was waiting for me to answer. I was dizzy with the need to kiss him, to celebrate Sophie, to feel as if I could have one normal night.

"How about we take this discussion to bed?"

"You want to talk?" His expression was neutral, and I knew if that was all I wanted, then he'd be there to hug me and make everything feel okay. I didn't need that tonight, and I pressed a kiss to his hand.

"No talking."

Chapter Twelve

Joachim

THE HEAD RUSH FROM ALL MY BLOOD LEAVING MY HEAD and rushing to my dick nearly made me woozy. I managed to keep enough of my senses to pull Isaac into my arms and claim his mouth in a kiss that was territorial as hell. His tongue slid over mine with equal passion, his hands roaming down my sides then to my ass. His grip was firm, his fingers biting into my glutes. Lust roared through me clouding my thoughts as I ground my cock into his belly. He moaned. A low, soft sort of sound that went directly to my balls. The kiss went on and on. I maneuvered him around, unwilling to break us apart for fear that if we stopped some new and terrible tragedy would arise. My dick would be incredibly sad if we had to postpone where this was leading.

"Mm, bed," he whispered when, finally, we had to come up for air. I nodded, then went back to kissing him. This went on for a full ten minutes as we sucked and nibbled at each other's mouths as if starved—which we both kind of were—only breaking apart to mumble breathy pleas for a bed before we returned to feasting on each other. I could kiss him forever. He fit so perfectly against me... in my arms...

"Joachim, I need you," he gasped when we next broke the surface for air like a couple of breaching whales. God knows my blowhole was twitching. I snorted at the thought and his eyes—now all black from his pupils being blown—widened.

"I was thinking about whales. Never mind. I need you too." Cupping his face, I licked into his mouth, crushing my lips over his puffy ones. We fumbled around the house, bouncing off furniture and a few walls, mouths fused, until we tumbled into the master bedroom. "Clothes. Off. Now." I grabbed the hem of his sweater and pulled it over his head. Static flashed in his hair, flaring madly and crackling like a green log on a fire. "I wish I had a fireplace so I could lay you down in front of it," I murmured as my hands moved over his chest. He was lithe yet firm, his chest sprinkled with whisps of hair that thickened as it traveled into the waistband of his jeans. "I think you would be glorious with firelight dancing over your flesh."

"Floors are overrated," he replied with a chuckle, then divested me of my shirt and belt. His fingers slipped into the curls on my chest. He flicked a nipple. I shuddered so he did it again, and again, and again.

"Those are hardwired to my cock," I ground out when he took one between his teeth and tugged. My dick leaped as a groan slipped out of me. "Do you like to suck dick?"

He ran the tip of his tongue around that sodden nipple

as his gaze burned into me. "I like it just fine," he said and fell to his knees to free my prick. Fingers skimming his ears, I watched as he unzipped my pants, then reached into my underwear. He wasted no time. His fingers gripped my dick and pulled it up and out of my briefs. "Beautiful," he whispered, pulling the foreskin back to suck the head. My hips twitched, my hands diving into his hair, the tingle of an orgasm tickling my balls.

"God…" I panted when he took me fully into his mouth. "It's been… shit. Long time and you look so pretty with my dick stretching your mouth…"

He hummed around my cock. My toes curled inside my shoes as my pelvis rocked up then back. I was not going to last. It had been far too long. His tongue danced over the tip of my dick, gathering up precum that he smeared on his pink lips, and I felt the white-hot bolts of my release igniting at the base of my spine.

"Shit… coming," I huffed and tried to pull away. Isaac grabbed my hips and guided me back into the hot, wet glory of his mouth. His gaze never left mine. "Oh yes," I managed to say before I shot down his throat. His eyes closed as he swallowed pulse after pulse. I held his head tenderly, my fingers resting atop the crown of his skull as my eyes rolled backward. I was barely done and he was on his feet, yanking my mouth down to his. He smeared my spunk over my lips and tongue as he humped my thigh. The taste of myself didn't turn me on, nor did I love it… it simply was.

"Your turn," I grunted, then fumbled with his pants, struggling with his zipper. He jumped in to help, looking down at his crotch at the same time I did. Our brows met with a thunk that made us both wince and hiss. Then laugh. "We're so graceful." I chuckled as I literally tugged his pants down over his lean hips, taking his boxers with them. His prick sprang up right into my hand. "Look at you," I said as I began stroking him. He leaned into me, his mouth on my throat, his hips rolling. My thumb slid over his cockhead, and he whimpered.

"Don't stop," he cried out, his fingers digging into my bare shoulders as he began fucking my fist. I did as my lover asked. I only stopped once to spit on my palm, then took him in hand once more. He came with a shout. Cum coated my belly, warm ropes of spunk dotting my abdomen and navel as he came undone in my arms. I nuzzled at his neck, saying little things that lovers say while in the throes.

"Ah God, Joachim." He sighed as the last tremors rolled through him. I lifted my head to nibble at his lips. "We never made it to the bed."

"Mm, the night is young."

"And so are we?" he asked with a hint of mischief that I found wildly hot. All I'd known of him so far was the tense, terrified Isaac, but now that his worry was lightening more of the playful side was showing. I adored that part of him. Seeing him slowly returning to the man I assumed he was before his world crumbled only reinforced the idea that my taking sole custody of Sophie was best for all involved. This glorious loving man in my arms would find himself again, hopefully with me in his bed. I would always be in his life whether we were lovers or not. Sophie would bind us forever.

"You perhaps. Me? Not so much anymore." I scooped

him up, then dropped him into the middle of my bed. The mattress swallowed him up, then I covered him with my body. He linked his arms around my neck, then pulled me down for a kiss. Cooling spunk smeared between us, but neither one of us seemed to care. I had plans for more body fluids to be exchanged so why fret now? Our kisses were languid now that some of the madness had been slaked. Tender sighs and soft words of praise and admiration passed between us as we made out, legs tangled, cocks starting to rouse as the tasting and caressing went on. Soon we were both rock hard again and Isaac was pinned under me, one leg resting on my lower back, the other splayed out to the side while I made a meal of his throat. He had the most incredibly sexy clavicle that I'd ever seen.

I began rutting, my prick sliding down over his hole. He writhed under me, his dick pressed tightly between us, oozing precum to make slick trails. I toyed with a nipple, using my tongue to tease it into a hard peak as I flicked my hips.

"I have protection in the drawer," I mumbled against his warm flesh, raising my gaze from his chest to his face. His cheeks were flushed hot pink, his mouth open just a bit, and his eyes glowing like otherworldly sapphires. "I had a thorough screening before the stem cell transfer and all my tests came back fine." He made a slightly sour face that gave me pause. "Or if you don't like anal that's fine. Please don't let me push you into anything…"

"Mm, no, anal is amazing, I'm just not sure I can take that dick of yours," he confessed, which, of course, made me all puffy like a rooster for a moment.

"I'm sure I can get you ready for my dick," I replied, to which he gave me a look that could have been called daring. "Do you think I can't?"

"Well…" That was all he said, but those stunning eyes of his twinkled. Such a little mischief maker he was. I kissed his mouth hard and reached for a pillow. Once it was under his firm little ass, I took his ankles, pressed his knees into his chest, and told him to hold onto his calves, which he did with speed.

I sat back on my heels to admire the beautiful sight before me. There he was all spread out and open, his balls hanging heavy, his cock firm, and his tight little hole tempting me to work it—work him—into a froth.

Licking my lips, I placed a hand on each cheek, spread him wide, and buried my face in his ass. He yelped, then moaned as my tongue glided over his hole. I let my eyes drift shut as I rimmed him, reveling in the musky taste of him. I toyed with his pucker, licking and sucking and delving into him over and over and over.

"Joachim… I… ah, hell, oh shit so good… so good!" he rambled as I slid a finger in, then two, working them in and out, rubbing that small knot of nerves to make him scream out loud. His cock was red and leaking steadily.

"I'm going to fuck you now," I panted, kissing a path up over his balls, which I mouthed for a moment, then cleaned off his dick before leaving him for just a second to extract the condoms and lube from the nightstand drawer. "Do you want my cock in you now?"

"Yes, yes," he whimpered, his fingers white-knuckled as he clasped his legs to his chest.

A moan rolled from me. I hurried to get my cock

covered then slicked up. He begged for more when I worked some lube into his sweet, soft hole.

"You will get more," I assured him while moving along on my knees to position myself at his entrance. His pupils were fat, his chest covered with a fine sheen of sweat, and his cock hard as concrete. He was close, that was obvious. "Breathe, sweetness," I cooed as I pressed into him, my cockhead slipping through that tight barrier with ease. His mouth opened wide as his eyes drifted shut. I let my cock lead, stretching him as I sank into him right up to my balls.

"Fuck… fuck… oh fuck you fit," he cried out in a mix of shock and pleasure.

"I told you I would. God, you feel wonderful. So tight. So hot and tight." I pulled out and then sank back in. Isaac made a noise that sent shivers down my spine, so I repeated that movement. His back arched. I pulled out and thrust back in, nailing his prostate. His cock was purple and wet with precum. I took him in hand, then rocked in and out, making sure to get that secret spot with each flick of my hips. His orgasm hit him within moments, his cock spewing hot spurts of spunk that flew up to his chin. I drove it home, slamming into him over and over until my balls drew up tight. With a grunt, I buried myself in him as deeply as I could go, his heels driving into my ass, as we slid off the pillow. Holding him tight I rode out the orgasm, his eyes locked with mine. He clenched around me as he whispered naughty dirty things like "Fill me up" and "Give it all to me" while I pumped a load into the condom.

It took us both a moment to catch our breaths.

Isaac wet his lips, rubbed them together, and then said, "Wow" which made me snigger like a drunken goose.

"Yes, that… about covers it," I gasped, then rolled to my back, my cock sliding free. He came with me, his slight form sliding over my chest like a blanket. He kissed my chin then my mouth. I pushed his wet hair from his face, holding it back as I gazed into his eyes. "I like you a lot."

"I like you a lot too," he replied on a rustle of a whisper that did funny things to my belly. We smiled at each other like dimwits, obviously smitten beyond reason. "That was… wow."

"Mm yes, it was wow. Are you hurt? I was trying not to—"

He kissed me soundly. "I'm fine. Might not be able to sit down for long stretches tomorrow, but I'm fine. Next time, I top. If you're into that?"

"I'm into bottoming and a next time." His smile grew into a grin that made my sweaty skin tingle. My stomach chose that moment to growl like a bear. He patted my abdomen. "I'm also into showering and eating."

"Me too. Maybe next time will be after showering and eating?" My eyes flared. "It's been a long time," he stated with no remorse. He gave me a shrug and a smooch, then rolled off the bed with a moan. I lay there smirking until he hit me in the face with the pillow that had been wedged under his now sore ass. I sputtered and knocked it aside. He bolted. I sprang up and pursued him into the master bath, where I caught him and kissed him into the bathtub.

The shower curtain rattled on metal rings when we pulled it shut, his body tight to mine. The water was hot at first, too hot, and we danced a bit until we had it set. He washed me off, then I soaped him. We shared small talk and kisses as we toweled off and got dressed in sloppy house clothes.

Food was something simple. Fruit and a quickly made meat and cheese tray with assorted crackers. Ice-cold spring water to drink. We scurried back to my bed, him checking with the hospital to ensure that Sophie was okay. She was sound asleep the nurse assured us. I could feel the pull to leave this room and go to her. Surely Isaac felt the same. And we would end up back there soon I was sure, but perhaps we could sneak in just another hour.

I sat back against the headboard, watching him chow down on turkey kielbasa and cheese on round crackers as he told me story after story about his days in Florida, his sister, and the things they used to do as children. I was eager to hear about his past, for it was my daughter's past as well. He was bright-eyed and chatty, cracker crumbs tumbling from his well-kissed lips to the bedding. Not that I cared about a few crumbs. Covers could be washed. I simply wanted to sit here, feed myself and him, and listen to him talk. He was pink-cheeked and animated, telling me about various art projects he had started then had to set aside after his sister passed and he stepped in to raise Sophie. I could feel the longing in his voice. He missed creating. His comic strips were keeping him afloat—barely —but he could do so much more with his life and talent, if he had the time and freedom to do so.

And that was something that I could help with. After chewing a cracker with a thick slab of cheddar and kielbasa, I took a swig of water then patted his knee. He smiled sweetly at me, popping a wheat cracker into his mouth.

I think I fell for him at that moment.

Hard.

Chapter Thirteen

Isaac

THIS CONNECTION HAD BEEN BUILDING SINCE THE FIRST day I saw Joachim. Hell, I'd been attracted to him even with the worry and fear I carried inside me, despite the pain and the caring for Sophie. But what we'd done had pushed past me being scared and had left me vulnerable, and it was that vulnerability that meant I was talking too much.

"Sorry," I said around the cracker. "I kind of get lost when I'm talking about my art."

"I love it," he said and stole a kiss before settling back to eat.

"Nick called me again." I needed to get the subject off my art to something where we could chat together, as opposed to him listening to me rambling on. We shared a wariness of Nick Sinclair. The owner of the Rebels was a shrewd man with an eye for promotion, and Sophie was the very best kind of publicity. Who couldn't fail to buy into the story of a child being saved by a player on the team? There was already a campaign to raise money for the hospital in her name, and the way the money was rising they'd be able to build a new wing.

"Just ignore it, and he'll go away," Joachim murmured and wiped a stray crumb from his impressive chest.

"I wouldn't know what to say anyway. I guess I could talk about Sophie and her being ill in general terms, but I won't talk about Ashley or the cancer, and I know I'd trip over questions about you."

"You could just tell everyone the truth. I don't think there's anything wrong you could say right now. It's obvious how much you love Sophie."

"Anyway, I said no. He wants photos of her coming out of the hospital, told me you'd agreed he could have one photo of you and Sophie, but not showing her face."

"The fundraising is at two million already. It could do a lot of good for kids like Sophie, and I didn't think it would hurt."

"No, it doesn't, but I won't let Sophie be exploited."

"I'm her dad," he said with a smile, which turned to fierce determination. "I won't let anyone hurt her. Or you."

My heart beat a little faster. There was something about the way he spoke that made me feel precious and looked after. It was a scary emotion to have right now, given how vulnerable I felt sitting naked on the bed with Joachim. He'd stripped away part of my barriers, and I'd let him inside, and it was a truly frightening thing to think he could see those hidden parts of my fear and love.

"I have a new rule," Joachim took another cracker, "no talking about Nick Sinclair when naked in bed."

"I can get behind that one." I smiled, and Joachim grinned back at me.

"Tell me more about your art."

"You don't want to hear more of that."

"I do. What do you plan on doing next with it?"

"I have an idea for a comic book. It's something that's been in my head for ages. Superheroes maybe, like a school where you go to learn how to be a superhero, but you're taking math and all the other subjects at the same time. It would be young adult, or maybe new adult, I don't know yet."

"It sounds interesting."

"Superhero school has been done to death, but my idea is doing it with predominantly queer characters. So, that's something I need to do my research on, but I've already drawn up a storyboard for the first edition." Great, I'd gone back to yapping on about my art again. "You don't need to hear this, honestly."

"I'd love to help." He gave my leg a squeeze, then rolled to the side a bit, careful of the nearly empty cutting board we'd used as a makeshift charcuterie board. "I know that will take lots of time and money, so sign me up as a donor whenever you get it off the ground." He pulled open the dresser drawer, shoved the box of condoms aside, and pulled out a large white envelope. I didn't think anything of it, still caught up in the concept in my head to build on my strips and make them into something that could generate more money. If I earned enough, I could make a good life for Sophie, and I had images of this perfectly wonderful future that were so bright and clear they hurt. Joachim could visit us between games. We could visit

Boston, and yeah, the thought of moving to Boston was also right there front and center. Sophie and I could move in with Joachim and be a family.

"More help. I think what you've done for Sophie is enough." I was intrigued as he handed me the envelope. On the front the names Bailey, Morris, and Long Attorneys-at-Law were printed in embossed letters. It was the kind of envelope that came from a firm someone like me would never be able to afford.

"Open it." He sounded like a fond parent at Christmas handing over the best present and already thinking their kid was going to love what was inside.

"What is it?" I asked as I wiped my fingers on my T-shirt.

He gave me a shy smile and then waved a hand to indicate I should open it. "It's to help you secure all those dreams of yours that you shoved aside so you could take care of Sophie."

I snorted a laugh. "Is it stuffed full of thousand-dollar bills?" I opened the envelope and peeked inside. "Damn it. No cash." I smiled at him, but he looked oddly stiff and there was caution in his eyes, so I went with my best teasing tone. "Just a bunch of formal looking papers."

"They're *your* copies of papers from my lawyers."

"Copies of what?" I pulled out the stack of legal vellum all nicely paper-clipped with tiny flags for signatures here and there. I scanned the top sheet, but I wasn't really reading the words, just seeing Sophie's name and my name and a ton of big words *pursuant to this* and *State of Massachusetts that*. I waited for him to give me a summary. Was it a trust for Sophie? That was a good thing.

Joachim had money, not as much as he used to, I got that, but enough so it was right and good that he should set up a trust in his daughter's name for when she was older. "What are they for?" I asked. "Does this have to do with Sophie? Like a college trust?"

He smiled, but the smile didn't quite reach his eyes—if anything he suddenly seemed nervous and my chest tightened, panic began to creep in at the edges of my euphoric mood. Abruptly, I felt as if the papers detailed the end of my world and fear hit me so hard it stole my breath. I couldn't stop the sudden panic because it was rising so fast that I couldn't talk.

"Once I sign on all the dotted lines, you won't have to worry about taking responsibility for Sophie. I'll be her father, sole guardian and provider. Legally. Then we can work on what comes next."

"What?" Oh God no. Whatever small flicker of love had started to grow was extinguished immediately. I was going to lose the last person in my life, and it was him taking Sophie from me.

He looked confused, and his smile dropped a little. "Well, I will be once the family court approves my petition."

"How can you..."

"Then you'll be free to return to your life. No worries, no bills, no sick child to worry about." He sounded so earnest as if he was the one doing me the favor. Was he taking Sophie and telling me to go and live a life without her?

"No..."

He forged ahead, ignoring the fact I couldn't even

make words. "All of that will be for me to deal with. You'll be able to devote yourself to working on your career, living your single life."

"Sophie—"

As if he'd been practicing what to say and had a list in his head, he pushed on. "I hope you choose to stay here in Boston with us. I think we could make it work. But if you decide to go back south, I'll make sure I fly us down to see you during summer breaks." He paused then. What did he want me to say? *What did he want me to do?* Was he expecting me to throw myself at him as if I'd been given the greatest gift of my life? I stared at him, my vision blurring as if I was crying. I touched my face, staring at my damp fingers, the tears forced up from my heart— which he'd stabbed and slit open with his promises and his plans. He stared right back at me, love marks on his clavicle and crumbs on his lap, and then I saw him flinch.

He knew what he'd done.

He'd waited until he'd gotten me into bed, then he threw this at me as if…

What?

Did he think sex was enough to blur the edges? I started to tremble, adrenaline coursing through me, fresh tears spilling from my eyes, and my heart… God, my heart… it was breaking. I scrambled back off the bed, not knowing which way was up, grabbing my lounge pants, vulnerable and open to his gaze before I yanked them on and found my shirt.

"No!" I snapped, reaching for the legal documentation, and pulling off the first few sheets, ripping them, the paper clip catching and staples stopping me from tearing it all. In frustration, I gathered up all the pieces, and I saw him move from the bed as I backed out of the room. I needed matches. If the papers didn't exist, then he couldn't cut me out of Sophie's life. I panicked as I yanked open the first drawer and slammed it shut when all it held was cutlery.

"What are you doing?" he asked, touching my arm.

I shoved him away. The second drawer held nothing, the third had candles, and right there, matches.

"Isaac, stop."

I thrust the paperwork in his kitchen sink, blocking access with my body as he tried to reach past me, and lit a match, dropping it on the paperwork.

Another match.

Another.

I wouldn't let anything destroy my connection to Sophie. My parents were gone, my sister too, and I'd only just got Sophie back.

"Jesus Christ, Isaac!" He forced his way past me to get to the tap. I wouldn't let him, ramming him away, but he was an immoveable object. I couldn't stop him from turning on the water, the flames extinguishing until there was a pile of charred and sodden paperwork and the acrid smell of melted plastic and smoke. The smoke alarm sounded, and he moved away from me, grabbing the matches and a dishtowel, waving the towel under the alarm until it silenced.

And through all of it, I stood at the sink and stared at the mess.

"Isaac, talk to me."

For the longest time, I watched the papers wrinkle in the moving water, then I very deliberately took a handful of them and shoved them in the garbage disposal before turning it on. Then another. And another.

He didn't try to stop me, and only when every shred of the paperwork was gone, did I turn to face him.

"Was getting me into bed part of the plan?" I asked, my voice cracked, and I realized I was still crying. Where was all this anguish coming from?

"No. What plan? I don't understand."

The worst thing, the very worst thing of all, is that he stood there as if he was completely innocent, as if he never calculated everything to get to this point.

"I was falling for you... I actually had feelings... then you get me into your bed, you act nice, make it sound like you're giving me the freedom to be my best self, even when you know... you *know* Sophie is my entire life."

"Stay here then, and we can make a family of sorts. That sounds perfect. I'm confused. I mean I never expected you to leave, you have to understand that."

A family of sorts? Why did that make so much sense? He was right in saying that I could stay here, maybe even in this house, be an uncle and play a part in Sophie's life, so what was wrong with me?

"Sole custody?" I snapped. "You want to cut me out of Sophie's life, destroy the only connection she has to her mom, the same woman you fucked and left like she was nothing at all." Christ, now I'd tipped over into drama.

He paled. "That wasn't what happened. I didn't know. I was—"

"Drunk. So fucking drunk you don't even recall making the most perfect thing on earth?"

"That's not fair—"

"If you think for one minute, I will let some second-rate alcoholic jock take *my* daughter, then you're wrong." I know I was yelling and part of me reveled in hurting him, years of worry and pain building to this moment where he thought he could manipulate me.

"Recovering alcoholic—"

"Fuck you!"

"And I'm not second rate. I could have a contract for—"

"No!"

Hurt flared in his expression, and he stumbled back as if I'd physically shoved him, his hand on his chest.

Good, see how it hurts?

"She's not *your* daughter." He sounded confused, but there it was, a flash of anger in his eyes—what I thought might be a gleam of possession—and that was what I needed to see. I wanted him angry. I wanted him to fight this so I could pour all my fears into screaming back at him. My heart hurt, my stomach churned with fear, but it was despair that consumed me.

"Where were you when Ashley was pregnant?" I stormed past him and into my room, yanked out her journal, and turned to see he'd followed me, so I opened the book and searched for the entry. "Went to see HG, he looked right through me, offered me an autograph." I tossed the journal on the bed.

"She came to tell me?" He looked confused. "I didn't know."

"You looked right through her—"

"She didn't say anything—"

"Just because you fucked some girl at a party, doesn't

mean you get to be a daddy to Sophie and cut me out like I'm nothing."

"I'm not doing that." He sunk to the bed. "I thought you'd be happy with…"

I was so lost in my temper that I couldn't even feel compassion at the distress on his face.

"Happy would be you saying that you honor what I've been to Sophie, and that you wanted to work with me. Shared custody, not sole."

He tilted his chin and a stubborn expression showed me that wasn't what he wanted.

"She's my daughter, and I want the best for her."

"I work hard for her—"

"You have nothing to give her—"

"Excuse me?"

"No, I didn't mean that. I meant that I want her to have security and financial stability. I want to give her more than you are able to." He stood up, facing me head on. The fight was out of control, and I wasn't even sure why it had gotten to this point. All I knew is that we were hurting each other, throwing knives and hoping something drew blood.

"Better with me, someone who loves her and she knows, than with an alcoholic whose career is nearly done."

We were in each other's faces.

"I love her!" he defended.

"How can you? You don't even know her."

"I do. I'm her father—"

"You're a sperm donor," I threw at him.

He tensed, and for a moment, I felt fear. He was bigger

than me, stronger; he played a contact sport where hurting people happened on a nightly basis, and I was provoking him. We were both breathing heavily, but it was he who broke the impasse.

"What else did the journal say?"

That question threw me. He was tracing the pattern on the front of the book, and could pick it up and read it for himself. Only he didn't. He held back and respected the fact this wasn't his to read. Compassion tried to still the fire inside me, but then, just as quickly, it vanished, and I hardened my heart. He wasn't going to take Sophie from me as if I didn't matter, as if I didn't think of myself as her dad, as if she didn't call me daddy.

"That you partied, that you were drunk, that you looked right through her, that she felt used, that she almost gave up when she realized she didn't want a baby."

He went white then, his eyes wide. "She didn't want Sophie?"

"She wanted a baby one day, but with someone who cared. Only the moment she heard a heartbeat she was in love with her baby, and it was *me* who promised I would be the best dad that Sophie would ever have. Sophie is only here because Ashley fell in love with the baby growing inside her and knew I would take care of them."

He looked defeated. "I just want to make things right now."

"How? By handing the only father Sophie has ever known legal documents releasing him from responsibility and calling it a good thing."

He winced. "I just want the best for Sophie."

I picked up my cell phone and dialed the emergency

number that Nick Sinclair had given me. The Rebels owner was all *call me whenever*, so I was damn sure doing this. I didn't even give Nick a chance to talk.

"I want a car picking me up from Joachim's house. Now. I want a suite in the hotel next to the hospital. I'll do your interview, but in return, I want access to the best lawyer your team can get me, otherwise I will fuck everyone over in that interview—you, the team, Joachim, everyone. I will paint the worst fucking canvas of hell, if you don't get that lawyer in my suite by the end of tomorrow."

Nick blustered, started to ask questions, but I ended the call and began to shove things in my backpack.

"You don't need to leave," Joachim pleaded and gripped my arm. "Please, I'm sorry. I didn't think this through."

"No you didn't."

"Surely, it's for the best. I mean, I'm just focusing on Sophie and what if she needs medical help again? I have some money, and my blood, I can donate—"

I yanked my arm away. "She'll have me."

"Shit, Isaac."

I shoved past him, with not much in my bag but the essentials, then stalked to Sophie's room, shoveling clothes into her case, diapers, knowing most of her stuff was at the hospital, including her beloved B-Bear. He even followed me in there.

"This is stupid." Joachim carded his hands through his hair. I zipped the case shut and headed for the door.

"No. This is me fighting to keep my place in Sophie's life—"

"You're her uncle, you'll always be there—"

"I expect I'll see you at the hospital in a few hours. Sophie will be coming to the hotel with me."

"I have practice. I want to be there. Can we pick her up later in the day? Isaac—"

I slammed the front door behind me, stalked to the sidewalk, and only had a few minutes before a town car pulled up at the curb. I expected him to try to talk to me, steeling myself for more pain.

He never even came out of the house.

Chapter Fourteen

Joachim

I'D NEVER BEEN TO THE JAMAICA BAY PART OF THE CITY before. It seemed like a good place. The bars were nice. I'd passed several. Was it just me or have those who were not recovering alcoholics ever noticed just how many bars there are in your neighborhood? Add in beer distributors and state stores and a man could find himself a cold one just about anywhere. I wasn't sure what that said about booze in our modern culture, and right now, that was a bit too highbrow of a concept for me to handle. Right now, I was focused on one foot in front of the other as I climbed the front steps to the address my sponsor had given me weeks ago. I rang the bell, waited, rang it again, and then glanced to the side when I saw two women scoping me out through a second-story window. Great. Now the cops would show up, and I'd have to explain why I was waking people up at ten minutes to one in the motherfucking morning.

Well, officer, I was having a moment of crisis and drove to, and parked in front of, at least ten bars before I somehow—perhaps by the grace of God—wound up in this fine, upstanding neighborhood seeking counsel from—

The door opened and it was not the lanky ginger wise-ass I'd assumed it would be.

"Joachim," Dan said around a yawn. "You look rough. Vic's just taking a leak. Come in." The short, dark-haired man reached out to take my arm and led me into their home. He then waved at the neighbors, I assumed, and shut his front door. "Have to let the neighbors know all's good here," he said with a sleepy, but warm smile.

"Yeah, you know how lesbians are," Vic said as he descended the stairs in flannel lounge pants and a Pantera T-shirt.

"Don't," Dan warned his spouse. "I'll go make coffee. Good to see you, Joachim. The team is looking good this year." He left after stealing a kiss from Vic.

"Cute as a button, isn't he?" Victor asked, and I nodded. Sure, yeah, Dan was cute, but he wasn't Isaac. Christ, what had I done? "You look like an old shoe someone's dog ate then shit out. You sober?"

"Just."

"Been there and bought the beer cozy." He looped an arm around my sagging shoulders. "Come on, Dan makes some frou-frou coffee, but it'll do. We'll talk. Shit will look better after we get you steady."

I let him lead me into a tidy kitchen with bright curtains and modern appliances. Dan was shoving a mug into a Keurig, the smell of coffee filling the homey area. I sat down with a huff, then rubbed at my eyes with my fingers until they watered. It had to be the rubbing making my eyes leak. Hockey players didn't cry.

"Hey, here you go." I lowered my hands and blinked at Dan pushing a cup of steaming coffee at me. "Cream is in the fridge. Sugar is in the bowl. If you want something to eat, Vic makes a mean egg sandwich."

"Thank you." I took the mug with trembling hands, then took a tentative sip of the French vanilla goodness. Dan patted my shoulder before he gave Vic a loving glance and left us to our work. And make no mistake, this was going to be laborious.

"It's not real sugar; it's that fluffy fake shit. Dan's anal about my sugar intake." Vic sighed, then sat down across from me. He took the lid off the sugar bowl and stirred a few spoons of sweetener into his coffee while I sipped at mine in silence. "So…"

"I fucked up everything," I blurted, lowering my cup before my quaking hands spilled some on my lap.

"Doubtful. I mean fucking up *everything* is monumental. You probably just fucked up one thing, and it feels massive," he replied, then took a sip and added another spoonful of sweetener. "Was the fuckup professional or personal?"

"Personal." I blew out a breath as my gaze skimmed over the pictures on the fridge. One of a blond teenager in goalie gear and one of a redheaded young man in what looked like a white wedding dress in the arms of a massive older man in a tuxedo.

"Those are my kids. BJ and Jackie Blue. My daughter

is going to Cornell to study to be an addiction therapist while playing on the Cornell women's ice hockey team. My boy Jackie is living in New York and works in fashion. He just got married to Martin, an ex-Boston fireman."

"You have a lovely family," I mumbled. "I think I've destroyed all hopes of having the family I wanted."

"I doubt that."

I shook my head. "I don't. God he was upset. Hurt and angry. The things we said to each other…"

"Yeah, heat of the moment cuts are always pretty deep." He blew into his coffee as the house settled into the middle of the night quiet where only the pipes knocked or the heater clicked on. "Why don't you give me the skinny on what went down. If you want. If not, we'll just sit here and drink my old man's French vanilla brew and talk hockey. Totally your call, my friend."

Generally, I disliked airing my dirty laundry, which was due in part to how I'd been raised, the old hockey player creed of not shitting where you slept and part of the addiction itself. If you hide your drinking, no one will know you're drunk. Only thing was they *did* know you were drunk.

"I thought I was doing the right thing," I began. Vic nodded so I dug deep and let it all out. And I do mean *all*. Even the sex bits. I didn't go into details, of course, but I did mention that we'd made love, and it had been incredible. Victor made some raunchy comment that made me snort, but the amusement died off when I relayed how things had crashed and burned after I'd given Isaac those damn papers.

"Oh, the humanity." Vic sighed into his now second cup of coffee. Neither of us were going to be able to sleep, not that I thought I'd rest tonight. This morning. Whatever. "Yeah, sounds like a real Hindenburg kind of situation." He leaned forward a bit, resting his forearms on the old table. There were gouges in the wood, paint speckles, and a chip from the edge that stood out. This table had seen some life. Two kids worth of living. Countless meals. Homework and coloring with crayons. Kitchen tables really did seem to be part of the heart of a home.

Why the hell are we waxing poetic on a damn table?

I snapped out of the fog I'd stumbled into. "All I wanted to do was make his life easier."

"Yeah, I see that." I zoned out again, staring at the gouges in the oak wood. Victor rapped me on the knuckles with his spoon. I startled. "I can also see his side. Sounds to me like your Isaac"—I did love the sound of *your Isaac* —"has devoted his whole life to his niece. I mean she calls him daddy, so that means he encouraged her to do so. Ripping her away from him isn't going to go down well."

"I'm not ripping her away! She's my daughter!"

"Whoa, settle down, Jokey." He raised his hands, palms up and out, and gave me a look that instantly took the vinegar out of me. I mumbled an apology. I really *was* all over the place. Fuck but a gin and tonic would taste so much better than this vanilla shit. Catching that last thought, I took a swig of coffee. "I know she's your daughter. But she's his too, you feel me?" I nodded sadly. "He's raised the tyke. He's been through all this fucking cancer shit with her. You're just this newcomer."

"Sperm donor. He said I was a sperm donor." Shit but that hurt more than I wished to admit. I was much more than that. I was Sophie's father.

"Well, for a few years, that's really all you were." I huffed, but bobbed my head. He was right. "So naturally, he's going to fall back on that kind of thinking when his world is being torn apart. Easier to revert to you being some unknown jerk of a drunk, then he can rail and rage at you without compunction."

"I don't want to be just a sperm donor. I want a family. I want to be a part of my daughter's life. Can he just take her away from me?"

Vic shrugged. "I don't know, man. I mean custody is a tricky thing, and neither of you are legally her pops, so who knows what will happen. Maybe the state will step in and take her into their care until the courts settle things?" The horror of that thought hit me like a cheap shot in the corners. "I'm not saying that's what'll happen, just that it might. What did old Doc Strange say about a million possible outcomes?" He scratched his long nose. "Maybe that was only about Thanos, who fucking knows? The point is that both of you have legit claims on Sophie, but in the end, Isaac is going to lose because you're the official father. What he needs to do is learn to deal with that reality now, and step back a bit."

"I want him in her life."

"Sure, as her uncle, not her daddy."

I frowned. It all sounded so simple when laid out in black and white. But life wasn't quite that simple. I felt that perhaps Victor didn't see shades of gray unless they were pointed out to him. "Look, this is all too complicated for a dunderhead like me. I know hockey. Outside of the rink, I know little. What we're here for isn't to talk custody. Let the lawyers do that. We're here to talk about your sobriety. And how epic it is that you came here instead of pulling up to a barstool and talking all this shit over with Johnny Walker."

"More of a Beefeater man. I *was* more of a Beefeater man," I quickly corrected.

"Good catch. So, you solid now or you want another cup? If I make it, it'll be plain old joe."

I glanced at the dark night, then held up my cup. "Plain joe is good."

I LEFT JAMAICA BAY AND DROVE RIGHT TO THE BARN FOR morning skate. If anyone noticed how shitty I looked, they didn't mention it. Until Moral showed up. He literally did a double take when he spied me lacing up my skates.

"You look like something my cat left on the carpet this morning," he announced to the whole dressing room. Xander stalked over to the bearded fool, linked his arm around his neck, and pulled him away. "What? I was just stating a fact. Ouch! You're tugging on my whiskers. Okay this is starting to turn me on, Cap."

Xander shoved him at his cubicle. "Sit. Meditate. Read a book. Just tone it down a little," Xander barked, then made his way out of the dressing room. I was eternally grateful for his running interference. I liked Moral. I really did, but he was just too robust for me now. I was running on zero hours of sleep, and we had a game tonight against my old team. Those were always tough as I'd made lots of friends on the team. Emotionally, it was going to be tricky without all the bullshit with Isaac.

No one said much to me during morning skate. I declined going to the coffee shop. I did not need to see Austin and his boyfriend making googly eyes or kissing each other. I was in no mood. After skate, I sent Isaac a text message begging him to talk with me. It went unanswered. I had so much to say to him because, after practice when I got to the hospital, I found out that Sophie had been discharged into her uncle's care.

"Why did no one call me?" I bellowed at the nurse. She stood her ground, her chin coming up, and I instantly felt contrite for yelling at her. This wasn't her fault. It was Isaac's and Isaac's alone. "Forgive me. It's been a long day. Thank you for your help."

I slunk off, anger and pain broiling inside me. Once I was outside, I fired off several texts to Isaac where I vented more than just my spleen. I raged at the man, calling him all manner of names, and then when he refused to reply, I called my lawyer. His receptionist put me right through.

"He's taken her from the hospital without my consent. Can he do that?" I asked my counsel. There was a lot of hemming and hawing from his end. "I just need to know if I can go get my daughter and take her home."

"I wouldn't suggest doing that," my attorney said. I might have vented a bit more right there in the parking lot. People leaving their cars gave me a wide berth. I threw myself into my car.

"I'm Sophie's father, I should be able to claim my own child."

"She's not yours legally yet. Plus, if you go storming over to that hotel, it's going to make you look like a madman. Which is rather how you sound right now. Out of control. We do not want the world to see you acting out. They'll whisper that you're drunk."

"I'm not drunk! I'm furious. *She's my child!*" I roared, grateful for the windows barring the sound of my rage from passersby. When his reply was cool, calm, and collected, I pounded on the steering wheel in utter frustration. It did nothing to work the emotions churning inside out. Sophie was my daughter, but it wasn't just that. I thought I'd made a connection with Isaac—even fancied myself falling in love, The disappointment inside me was like poison, and as my lawyer talked and talked, making perfect sense, in the end, he somehow convinced me to let Isaac keep Sophie for now. He would call Isaac and ask for visitation. If Isaac refused, then my lawyer would petition the court, which might bring family services in. He said he would make sure Isaac was aware of that possibility, and he was sure that whatever had soured things between us would be put aside to keep Sophie out of the system. *I thought I'd fallen in love. I wanted more than this.*

Why didn't he understand?

I reluctantly agreed with my lawyer's plans, went home, tried to nap, but couldn't, and spent the next few hours sitting on the floor of Sophie's room staring at the ceiling.

When game time rolled around, I was possibly not in the best frame of mind, but unless you were concussed or had a bone sticking out of your flesh, you were on the ice. That was just how sports was. I hit the ice seeking the scent of blood. Foolishly perhaps, I got my first lick in on Jamie Rowe, whom I'd always liked. I upended him in the corner behind our net and got called for boarding. When I went to the penalty box, I caught the dark glower from our new defensive coach. Brady had *not* liked me checking his little brother so brutally. I didn't feel too good about it either, if I was being honest.

Still, the energy I'd dissipated stopped the battle in my head between hate and affection for Isaac and what he was doing.

Or what I'd done.

Hell, I didn't know anything anymore.

Knowing I was shit tonight, I tried my best to keep a cool head when things started to get a little physical. Which always happened. We were a gritty team. So was Tampa. Jamie and I came together in the second period by the benches. He knocked me off my skates with a monstrous—and clean—shoulder check that made my fillings rattle. I landed in the opposition bench, right on one of my opponents' laps. Drewy—Phil Drewson—a totally nice guy with whom I'd played golf numerous times, laughed at me, then pulled off my helmet and held it up into the air.

Something inside me snapped. I was done with people taking what belonged to me away from me. I punched Drewy in the face. The whole bench retaliated. My team then leaped over the boards, and we had us a good, old-fashioned bench clearer, only it was taking place *on* the bench, so I wasn't sure what the term was. All I knew was that Drewy's nose got broken, and I took a shot to the side of my head that made me forget common math for a minute or two.

When all was cleared and the penalties handed out, I was given a game misconduct. Seems the refs disliked being called assholes. Who knew? I stalked to the dressing room leaving my team at a major disadvantage. I may have taken things out on the glove drying machine before I thundered into the men's room to douse my head under the spigot. Fuck my blades. I'd get someone to put new ones on when I played again. Which I was relatively certain would not be tonight.

Four minutes later, Brady exploded into the men's room, his hazel eyes snapping, his tie riding his shoulder. I stood there, head soaking wet, ass perched on a sink, waiting for the other shoe to fall.

"Are you drunk?" I knew that would be the first question. It was fair.

"I am not." *I thought I was in love, or at least there was something happening. I fucked it up, but I didn't drink.*

Brady tugged his tie back down over the buttons of his shirt. "I was kind of hoping that you were, then you'd have an excuse for being a total asshole. You cost us the lead."

"Sorry, Coach."

He stomped over to me and put his nose an inch from mine. "You don't look sorry. You look like a fucking petulant child. My daughters show better restraint. You're on the bench for the next game."

"Yes, of course. That's justified."

"You're fucking right it is! And whatever the hell devil

is inside you, I want it fucking exorcised before you show up here again. Do we understand each other?"

"Yes, I understand." He gave me a look of disgust, spun on his heel, and then slammed out of the bathroom. No one came in to check on me. That was wise. They probably knew I needed space.

And a priest.

Chapter Fifteen

Isaac

STANDING HERE, LISTENING TO THE OWNER OF THE REBELS team shout at me, I felt like a criminal. A broken hearted, emotional wreck of a man.

I'd deliberately gone to the hospital this morning when I knew Joachim wouldn't be able to go. Taking Sophie from there was totally my call, legalities notwithstanding she was in my care, and I was her uncle-who'd-taken-her-into-the-hospital, which trumped daddy-who-didn't-have-legal-papers.

Yet. He didn't have them *yet*, but I knew it wouldn't be long and then he could cut me out of Sophie's life as if I'd never even existed. It would all be my fault because I'd not only slept with Joachim, but I spun out so badly that I crashed and burned.

Why didn't I just take the papers and have a rational discussion with the man I'd just had sex with? What *should* have happened was us sitting quietly having a thoughtful discussion about each other's place in Sophie's life. But no, I'd seen red, and then—shit—some of the things I'd said. Calling him Sophie's sperm donor was just the icing on one hell of a shitty cake of shit. Burning the papers had been this visceral need to destroy the words on them, but what did it do?

What did I do?

"You don't get to blackmail me." Nick Sinclair was right up in my face, his eyes flashing with temper and his hands in fists. "I could destroy you for this." I winced but said nothing because he was right. The gazillionaire certainly had enough money to buy my destruction, and I had blatantly blackmailed him. He was a force of nature, and even though I bet he could sic someone on me after the blackmail I'd tried on him, instead he'd organized representation for me. The thin gray-haired lawyer currently shut in the bathroom where Nick had pushed him, was going to help me, but it wasn't done out of the kindness of Nick's heart—he was pissed. Emmet Hancock, lawyer extraordinaire, arrived this morning with a briefcase and files, and Nick right on his heels. I'd had a shit night's sleep, not left the hotel suite, and Sophie had slept through most of my meltdown, but in the heat of my reaction to Joachim's legal announcement, I'd threatened Nick on the phone, and now I was feeling the fallout.

"I'm sorry," I offered and glanced at the bedroom where Sophie slept, blissfully unaware I was fucking up everything out here.

He poked me in the chest. "I've made the biggest baddest hockey players cry for fucking me over, you hear me? Cry."

I swallowed. That sounded like some hardcore intimidation he was admitting to. Although I got the feeling some of it was blustering, I didn't doubt that the man could bring even the strongest person to their knees.

"You were the only person I could think of to—"

"Don't even go there." He poked me again. "You said and I quote 'I will fuck everyone over in that interview, you, the team, Joachim, everyone. I will paint the worst fucking canvas of hell' remember that?"

God, that didn't sound like something I'd say, but the shame of it was that I recalled every single word.

"I'm sorry—"

"How do you think that kind of threat would go down in family court? Threatening me, my team, Sophie's biological father, with a canvas of hell? I mean, how did you even think up that shit about hell?"

"I don't—"

"Because I'm keeping it for the next team meeting."

"You're going to tell the team what I said?" I suddenly felt lightheaded and sat on the nearest chair.

"No." He flicked my arm. "I'm impressed at the analogy, and I'm keeping it." He widened his stance, crossed his hands over his chest, and cleared his throat. "How does this sound for the next time the Rebels lose?" He pasted a fake snarl on his face and lowered his voice. "If you think I'm paying you to fuck up with this hell canvas then you're wrong," he announced, then looked thoughtful, "or maybe 'that game was a canvas of hell!' What do you think? Does it work?"

I was so confused and exhausted, and the flash and chaos of Nick Sinclair was messing with my head.

"I don't…"

"Yeah, I think the second one. Anyway the reporter I hired will contact you for a time, and I'm counting on you to give the interview of your life and not to fuck the team over."

I couldn't keep up with the change in direction. "I said I wouldn't."

"I'm also here to tell you that I'm giving you a pass on your threats to me and my team because your little girl needs at least one of you firing on all cylinders, and I'm not sure we can count on Löfgren."

Just the sound of Joachim's name made me wince. I had a ball of confusing emotions lodged in my chest. I thought I'd been falling in love, and that I'd known him enough to begin to form a future with him—pictures of the three of us being a family—but whatever love I'd felt had been diluted with fear and anger. The love that had been such a new possibility of something, had never been given a chance to become more.

"What's wrong? Is he okay?" Surely if he was hurt, he would have told me for Sophie's sake? Or maybe he was too hurt and hadn't been able to tell us?

Nick rolled his eyes. "Did you *see* last night's game?"

I scrubbed at my eyes. I hadn't watched it, couldn't bear to watch Joachim and recall how we'd connected so deeply, only for our differences to tear each other apart. I saw that the Rebels had lost to Florida and spent way too long wondering if it was a twisted analogy for what Joachim and I were doing, thinking maybe the Florida victory was a sign that I was going to win as well.

Win what? Who would win anything when it came

down to courts and lawyers? Lying in Joachim's bed I'd felt so much peace, and a future I could imagine so clearly had been tantalizingly close. It broke me that I'd lost it all in the space of ten minutes.

"I didn't watch the game." And surely if he was hurt it would have been headlines because that was as far as I read.

"Let's just say that Löfgren's lucky he's still a Rebel, and that he won't be one for long if he fucks up that badly again."

My chest tightened. "Is he okay? Is he hurt?" I didn't want to think of him being hurt without someone to look after him... without me and Sophie.

"Hurt? He's too far gone to feel hurt," Nick snorted, and then it hit me what that might mean.

"Was he drunk?" Had I messed up so badly that I'd broken Joachim's resolve? The devil on my shoulder immediately suggested that if he was drinking, then that meant I was automatically the better man. The angel in me cursed me with shame, and I buried my face in my hands, but I refused to lose control. Joachim was a good man, just misguided and messing up my life right now. I didn't want to be any kind of winner if it meant that he was going to hit rock bottom. *I don't want to hurt him.*

"He wasn't drinking; he was just on a tear." Nick sighed. "Look, Isaac, do you want some advice from someone who's seen things and done things they regret?"

I glanced up at him, and instead of a blustering team owner, Nick looked oddly vulnerable for a millisecond before the swagger and bravado was back. Far too quickly, the openness had vanished, but that tiny crack in Nick's confidence made me wonder if he carried as many demons as I did. Suddenly, he wasn't some rich guy with more money than sense, and power over an entire hockey empire —he was just a man. Same as me.

"Okay."

"Talk to him. Tell him how you really feel and work it out because Sophie is your everything, and you might *never* get a second chance."

"I don't know what to say to him."

He shrugged. "Not much I can do about the talking part, but for fuck's sake, will you fix this so my million-dollar skater actually fucking skates?" He loomed over me, "or maybe I destroy you and dump you in *the worst fucking canvas of hell.*"

"Okay." I winced, but then the dramatic sneer turned to a wide grin, and Nick chuckled.

"That line is so gonna work. I'm keeping it." He yanked open the bathroom door where Emmet was perched on the closed toilet clutching his files. "All yours."

As dramatically as Nick had arrived, he left, and it was just me and Emmet, plus a sleeping Sophie, and I had a head full of regrets and fears.

Emmet brushed off the seat of his pants and then took all the files to the table, spreading out papers and clicking a pen. He didn't seem fazed that he'd been shut in the bathroom, but I got the feeling Nick was unpredictable and Emmet was probably used to it.

"Mr. Bailey, let's get down to it."

I took a seat, then went back out to the kitchen for

coffee, then paced. It was only when I realized I was avoiding the inevitable that I sat down again.

"Our first concern is child protection," Emmet launched straight into it. "What we want to avoid is Sophie being surrendered to family services. So, first we need to file a notice of…"

I couldn't concentrate. The thought of Sophie being with strangers—would the courts really do that? Maybe if I apologized to Joachim, we could work this out. Maybe I should call him and say I was sorry. *But that would mean he'd think it was okay for him to take Sophie.* I didn't want him to take Sophie and cut me out of her life. I couldn't imagine living without her, so I had to fight for the rights I had, but what if fighting hurt my little girl? Joachim and I had connected. I was sure of it—at one point I'd even had thoughts of the two of us together–being fathers to Sophie. Hell, as I lay there in his arms, I'd pictured an entire future of the three of us against the world.

I'd fallen for him, or at least for the image of him I'd created in my head. He'd been a mix of sex and love and promises, and he was everything I thought I wanted. Then he'd pulled the rug from under me, and I was just left feeling as if he'd used sex as a way of getting me to agree to what he suggested.

"… in conclusion, what that means is—"

"No," I interrupted whatever Emmet was saying.

"Sorry?" He glanced up from whatever legal document he was explaining, and I shook my head.

"I need to talk to Joachim."

"I can certainly arrange mediation with—"

"No. I mean, thank you, but I want to talk to him alone. Can we reschedule this meeting?"

"I would be remiss not to mention that I won't endorse—"

"I know what you're going to say, but I have to think of Sophie. So can we pretend you don't know I want to see him?"

Emmet shuffled some papers into a neat pile, clearly giving himself time to think. "Off the record, Mr. Bailey, if this matter can be resolved without resorting to litigation, then you'll save yourself a lot of heartache…"

"However this plays out, I still have to petition for legal responsibility for Sophie."

He inclined his head. "Then I'll prepare the documentation we need for filing."

"Thank you."

"I'll be in touch."

As soon as he left, I headed straight into the bedroom, sat on the edge of my bed, and watched Sophie sleep peacefully. The hospital had issued a long list of instructions, but her pain seemed like a distant memory as she smiled in her sleep. There would be a lot of medical visits, but I couldn't stay in this hotel room forever. Despair slowly won over hope. There was no reason to think that she would fall ill again, they were confident she was clear of cancer, but there was always a fragility about her that terrified me.

"I can't lose you, Sophie."

At some point in the night, she'd tossed B-Bear out of bed, and I picked him up and held him tight. He smelled faintly of the hospital, where they'd sanitized him, and it made me smile knowing that he was home now with her. I tucked him in the bed next to her, then kissed her forehead.

"Don't worry, sweetheart, I'll fix this."

Was I being selfish? Maybe I should step back and just be an uncle who visited on the holidays?

I promised Ashley that I'd look after Sophie forever.

I took my cell to the small kitchen, stared at it for a while before connecting to Joachim. I was torn whether I wanted him to answer or not, but was relieved when it went to voicemail, until I heard his message.

"Hi, this is Joachim. You know what to do." Sense memory of the way he held Sophie, of him smiling at her, loving her, then the moments we'd had in bed where everything seemed possible, all crowded my head. I chickened out of leaving a message and hung up, then counted to fifty before calling again, ignoring the message, and leaving my own.

"We should talk." I added the hotel details, the room number, and then texted him the same information as well. No way could he say I hadn't told him or extended a hand of reconciliation.

Sophie woke soon after, and desperate to get out of the room, I took her to the hotel restaurant for lunch, selecting a table in the far corner and ordering a little bit of everything I knew she loved to eat. Her appetite was better now, but still wasn't perfect.

"Daddy. Is B-Bear better now?" she asked between one bite of an apple and another.

"He's much better," I said and patted B-Bear on the head.

"Will he get sick again?"

My heart stopped, the fear coiling in my chest and stealing my breath. She was reverting to the moments when I explained to her how she was ill by speaking through B-Bear. Long moments of her not understanding why she felt so tired, or why she couldn't go out to play, or why she didn't have loads of friends like television-Dora had.

"He won't get sick again." I settled in that gray area between a lie and a truth. The prognosis was good for Sophie. She was cancer free. She was getting stronger every day, and she *would* grow up to do everything she wanted to.

Maybe she'd be able to do more with Joachim? Am I the best person for her? Was I just put in her life to see her to this point? Why had I spun myself a happy ever after with her and Joachim?

Why had I felt as if I could love Joachim?

We stopped by the gift shop, bought some treats and a stuffed unicorn that Sophie decided was going to be the best of friends with B-Bear, and we headed back to the room. Somehow, even though he hadn't answered my message, I sensed that he'd already be at the room, and I wasn't wrong. Leaning on the wall, Joachim straightened, grinned widely at Sophie, then crouched and held out his arms. Sophie danced into his hug, taking B-Bear and her new unicorn with her. I watched as Joachim picked her up and swung her around. He looked handsome, strong, but held her so gently that she would hardly feel it, and my stupid heart filled with warmth that was quickly replaced by sadness. The words we'd thrown at each other had formed a barrier between us, and I wasn't sure it'd ever drop.

We could have done so much together, the three of us.

"You made it," I murmured, just for something to say.

"You knew I would," he replied. His tone was even; he didn't sound pissed or regretful. *Was he feeling anything at all?*

"Look what I got, Papa J!" Sophie announced and waved the new unicorn under Joachim's nose. "This is Pink," she announced. "She's friends with B-Bear."

He sent me an anguished look, and I was just as broken. I'd never heard her call him Papa J. We hadn't told her directly who he was to her, but somehow, she'd known, or he'd filled a space she identified as Papa. Joachim stroked Pink, then B-Bear, and then Sophie in turn, and neither of us said anything about Papa J.

"I got you a present," he announced and handed her a bag in Rebels colors with the team logo on the outside.

"How about we get inside before we open it," I suggested, opening the door for us, and closing it against the world once we were in, while observing Joachim interact with Sophie. *With his daughter.* I could see him in her smile, in the way her eyes lit up as she pulled out notebooks and enough colored pencils to open a stationery shop.

"Can I draw now, Daddy?" she asked me, but it was Joachim who helped set her up at the table with all her coloring supplies, sitting with her and coloring with her, chatting about how she was feeling, how B-Bear was feeling, and most of all telling her he'd missed her. I tried not to listen, or watch, but I couldn't take it away from him that he was good with her. Of course, he was. I knew that he loved her. He'd saved her life, and she meant everything to him.

"You want coffee or something?" I asked when the staring became weird and the worry unbearable. He glanced at me, his smile dipping.

"Yeah, thanks."

I headed to the kitchen and took a few moments to gather my thoughts. Losing myself in the mindless task of selecting pods, recalling Joachim loved simple black coffee.

"I left her coloring," he said from behind me, and I let out a sigh. I needed to say something here, apologize, move this along, explain how he'd shattered all the stupid fantasies I'd created of us being a family, or how sex for me meant something. But basically, it all boiled down to one thing—I'd overreacted. I'd lost my shit, Sophie was the important one, and I owed him something for that.

"I never asked her to call me Papa J," he said when I didn't answer.

"I know you didn't."

"But she should know who I am. If it's okay with you, I *want* her to know for real who I am. Now that she's well I mean."

Of course, he was right, and when it came down to it, Sophie was the one at the center of this, and she should know for real that Joachim was her father.

"I'm sorry for everything I said," I murmured after a pause, then turned with the coffee and caught his surprised expression.

"I'm sorry too." He sounded so relieved, taking the

coffee from me before placing it on the counter. "I tried to tell you that before."

I raised an eyebrow. "What you actually left me was a ton of messages that weren't at all about you being sorry."

He closed his eyes briefly. "I know. I was angry, lost." He scrubbed at his face. "I was fighting... I thought I needed to drink. All I wanted to do really was talk."

"Talk?" I shook my head. "You want to take everything from me."

"I didn't mean it that way." His eyes were bright with emotion, and I fought the need to drag him in for a hug. "I'm not just a sperm donor, Isaac."

"I know," I admitted.

He leaned on the counter, with his hands thrust in his pockets. "I want to be a good dad."

I stifled my anger, tried to focus on how we should be agreeing about things so we could protect Sophie. "I've *been* a good dad since the day she was born."

He winced. "I want more," he added. "I want you in our lives as well."

Something about the way he said that, pushing me outside the circle, made me tense. "See, there you go, talking about me being this add-on in yours and Sophie's life. I'm more than that, I'm not just a random uncle who shows up for birthdays or Christmas. I've earned my right to be her daddy, and she loves me."

"Move in with me, permanently. Stay with me, and we can raise her together."

Hope flared in my chest. "And you'll stop the moves to become her father legally?"

He frowned, and I knew what he was going to say.

"Why would I stop the legal side? I *am* her father, and I need to protect that."

"Protect her from me, you mean?" I snapped.

"No, shit. No, protect her from the world, with my name—"

I held up a hand to stop him, then stepped closer and ignored the flash of concern in his expression. "And there it is. You're the alcoholic jock who thinks he can get whatever he wants without considering how it affects anyone else. Isn't that what you do?" The barbs hit home, but he pulled himself together.

"*Recovering* alcoholic, and I don't see how this affects you—"

"And that's your issue. I agree to this, and you get legal status, and I get nothing. Then you throw me out of your house, and what do I have then? What does Sophie have? She knows me as her daddy, she's all that matters to me, and I won't just lie down and let you walk all over us."

"I'm not trying to." He hunched in on himself defensively.

Neither of us were going about this the right way. "I've instructed my lawyer to petition for legal status."

"That's your right," he said after a pause, and I stared right into his amber eyes. "Maybe we could—"

"All that matters now is that we present a united front so that Sophie isn't taken away from either of us."

He reached out and pressed a hand to my face. The warmth of his hand branded my skin, although I flinched at first, I couldn't move. "Sophie first. But then, what about us?"

I placed a hand over his and pressed it slightly. "There can't be an us."

I pushed past him and went into the sitting room where Sophie had fallen asleep with her face on the drawing.

"Why?"

"I'm not losing someone else that I might care about. So, I think you should go."

"You care, wait, I want to tell her—"

"I'm being interviewed tomorrow. I'll send you the details, come back then, and we'll show a united front."

I scooped up Sophie and went into her room. He followed me, kissed her on the forehead, and we didn't say another thing to each other. When he left, he took my hand.

"You said you care, so what happened between us—"

I shook my hand free before I did something I regretted, like pulling him close and never let him go. "I care about Sophie, not you," I lied.

Seems as if lying was my default for now.

Chapter Sixteen

Joachim

I DIDN'T EVEN KNOW WHY I WAS IN THE REBELS PRIVATE room at the coffee shop.

When I'd left the hotel, I was at loose ends. We'd not solved a damn thing, let alone sorted out or explained about me being Sophie's father. Yes, she had called me Papa J and while that was all I'd dreamed it'd be, I wanted her to know me for real—the true me, her father. Isaac had asked me to come back tomorrow, and I damn sure would. I could go back now filled with anger and confusion, plant my ass on a chair, and simply refuse to leave, but that would solve nothing. I didn't want Sophie to pick up on the anger, blame sharing, and/or the chaos that was surrounding us. When the call came from Austin to meet them at Bean Town Brews I went. Only because I hated the loneliness of my home. It was empty without Sophie and Isaac. Also, a coffee shop wasn't a bar, so go me. Vic would be so proud when I told him. He'd pat my head and give me a slice of pie.

So, amid all the turmoil, I was doing okay. With the drinking at least. The rest of my life? That was up in the air.

"Oh! Dirty twenty!"

I blinked back into my surroundings at Mason's yelp. We were gathered at a table in a back room that was covered with manuals, papers, pads, pencils, character sheets, a grid map that had tiny figurines and monsters, coffee cups, and dice. Austin was hidden behind a folding board that I'd been informed was a dungeon—or game—master's board. Xander kissed his man on his lips as the others playing hooted in glee. Moral, Renco, Xavier, Robbie, and me. Then all eyes landed on me.

"I'm sorry. I drifted off. What are we doing?" I picked up a twenty-sided die and rolled it because that seemed to be what we did in this game. There was a lot of dice rolling.

"We're in the middle of a battle with this fire elemental," Austin, wearing what looked to be a sorting hat, informed me. Again. My head was not into this thing at all.

"Right, yes, the fire elemental." I tried to avoid Xander's worried perusal and focused on the bright red die with the yellow numbers that I'd just rolled. I winced. "Nat one."

"Ouch," Xavier moaned. His dark brown gaze worried behind his designer eyewear. Did he even really need glasses? "If my math is right one hit from the elemental is going to kill you."

We looked at Austin as he tried to appear nonplussed. He failed miserably. As soon as I heard his die hit the table, I knew I was toast. Paladin toast, extra crispy. Which was probably for the best as my head was not into fantasy role-playing.

"Yeah, that was a critical hit. Sorry, Joachim."

Moral patted my back as if I'd just lost a pet. These guys took this Dungeons & Dragons thing *really* seriously.

"I cast the cantrip Spare the Dying!" Robbie called out. I shook my head. Everyone at the table gasped. "But you're dead, my man," Austin's boyfriend—our cleric—said, then pointed to my little mini paladin lying face down on the grid map. Austin had flicked him over after the killing blow.

"Let me lay there. I'm not really into this game right now, and I'm fucking up things for the rest of you. I'm going to go home." I gave them a weary smile, rose, and made my way to the coat rack. The coffee shop was packed, as it always was on game night, with all eyes now on me shrugging into my coat. I just needed to get out into the chilly air to clear my head. With a wave I ducked out, the cool night enveloping me. I had taken maybe twenty steps when someone jogged up and passed me, bumping into my left arm.

"On your left," Xander called, then slowed from a jog to a walk. "Always wanted to say that."

I smiled at the *Captain America* reference, shoved my hands into my coat pockets, and stalled my walk.

"You didn't have to leave the game," I said as Xander wrapped his arms around his middle. "Go back inside where it's warm and kill that monster."

"We all decided it was time for a coffee break." He hurried to zip his jacket. "Man, fall is coming fast and early. Can you feel winter on the air?"

"Mm-hmm." I stood there staring at him, my car just a mere hundred feet or so away. "Xander, you don't have to do this."

"Do what? Worry about a friend and teammate? What kind of captain, or buddy, would I be if I just let you wander off into the dark Boston night? What if you ended up in the harbor?"

That made me smile and I recalled the photo on Vic's refrigerator of his son's husband. "If I fell into the harbor maybe a handsome Boston Marine Firefighter would pull me out. I've seen pictures of one, he's a handsome bastard."

"Right. Well, being given mouth-to-mouth by a hot BFD fireman aside…"

"Chasing down sullen teammates is not part of your job as captain."

A car rolled by, and someone shouted our names followed by a "GO REBELS!" chant. We both lifted a hand in recognition.

"Actually, part of my job as captain *is* to make sure all the players are happy and not floundering in the harbor or lying dead in the Enchanted Forest of Palomar. Seriously, Brady said so." I snorted. Xander gave me a lopsided grin, the same one that made all the lady fans swoon, and some of the male fans as well. "Is it Sophie?"

"No, no, she's doing well. Incredibly well. Isaac and I are cautiously optimistic."

"Great! That's awesome. Uh… is it the urge to uhm…"

"Drink? No more than usual."

"Okay, so it's you and Isaac and your *thing*?" I shook my head. There *was* no *thing*. There was no us. Just ask Isaac. He made it incredibly clear that we were done. I had to accept that and move on. What we'd had was just an aberration. A glimpse into a future that could have been, but now wasn't. A future that was as dead as my poor paladin.

"There is no *thing*," I blurted out, then glanced skyward. The city lights made it impossible to see any stars.

"Oh. I'm sorry. We all kind of thought that you and Isaac seemed to be growing closer. Did something happen?" I shrugged and pulled my lips over my teeth. "Right, okay, well I won't push, but if you want someone to talk to you have my number."

"Thank you." I lowered my gaze from the night sky to my captain. A man whom I admired greatly on and off the ice. "Sometimes we just don't get what we want in life, yeah?"

"I don't know about that. I think that if we fight hard enough for the important things, the things that *really* matter, we can have what we want in life. You just can't give up."

"What if we don't know what we want?"

"Then you need to figure it out before your future is lying face down in a steaming pile of fire elemental poop."

"Is that where I am? Facedown in monster feces?"

"Yep." He popped the P.

"Well shit."

"Literally. We'll let Robbie cast his healing spell on

you and then when we play again you can join us if that's what you want. If not, we'll say you left on a solo quest to find your heart's true desire."

We paused in our discussion when Renco hustled past, his hood drawn up over his head, without uttering a word to us.

"Must be time to go home and curl up with his stick," Xander commented off-handedly.

"Goalies," I replied as if that explained our netminder's odd behavior. And it kind of did…

Xander clapped my shoulder, then hustled back into Bean Town Brews to rejoin our friends and his boyfriend. I ambled to my car, then flopped behind the wheel, hands cold, staring into the back seat via the rearview at my daughter's car seat. If there was one thing that I knew I wanted it was Sophie. That was never in question. And perhaps that would be enough. Maybe after some time what Isaac and I had been building would wither and die. We'd move on, each of us living out our lives as the fates dictated. Sharing time with Sophie and enjoying a friendship. We could do that. We could be friends. For Sophie.

So, you're going to lie to your little girl?

"No, not lie just…" I exhaled, then let my brow thud to the steering wheel. Sometimes I loathed my inner voice. It had led me down so many dark paths. Why was I listening to it now?

Because your inner voice and your demon are two different things, Joachim.

Okay. He had me there. "Adults lie to children all the time. We tell them there's a Santa Claus and an Easter

Bunny. We tell them that their hamster went to live on a farm with its mom and dad." Inside my head was quiet. "Yeah, I got you on that one."

Now that he was silent, I could think. Xander's words rattled around inside my skull all night, making sleep nearly impossible. Morning skate the next day was dismal. Brady worked me hard. It was a well-deserved raking over the coals. Nothing like wind sprints to let a player know how pissed off his coach really was.

It took me an hour on the massage table to get my calves and thighs to stop cramping. Rory, the new masseur, was spent by the time we were done, he'd put so much into making me loose.

It was all for naught it seemed because as soon as I arrived at Isaac's hotel room at the assigned time, all the tension was back tenfold. He greeted me at the door with a fake smile.

"Katie Long is already here." I blinked stupidly. "She's from *Hockey World News*? Nick sent her over to do a human-interest piece on our family now that Sophie has had her transplant."

"Family? Did you tell her that there would be no family?" I asked in a heated whisper. His face tightened. "Sorry, that was low."

"It's okay, we just need to get through this so the world can see that we're solid and we don't lose Sophie to care."

"That will happen over my cold, dead, paladin body," I growled low and deep.

"Paladin?"

"Not important."

"We should talk to Sophie first, tell her about you."

I didn't expect that. At all. "Okay."

I threw back my shoulders, wishing I'd taken more care after my shower. Since it was just morning skate, we had no suit and tie requirement, so I was in jeans and a Rebels fleece sweatshirt. Isaac nodded tightly and stepped aside to let me in. As I passed, I picked up the smell of his body wash. My body reacted instantly, a small nugget of yearning unfurling low in my belly. He looked so good. His hair was tidy. His shirt played well with his coloring, and his jeans were pressed. I fisted my hands until my nails dug into the flesh to keep from touching him.

Sophie looked up from playing with some blocks when we entered the living area of the suite. She shot to her feet then ran to me. Her dress was pink and frilly, and her eyes glowed with happiness. If only Isaac's and mine did as well.

I gathered her up, kissed her cheeks several times, which made her giggle, and then I went over to shake hands with the pretty brunette in the rust-toned dress. There were lights set up in here, along with a photographer whose name was Bob. Great. Pictures. I'd have to be extra careful not to let any sign of melancholy or distress show as the interview went on.

"We need a while," Isaac told the interviewer and then tugged me into the bedroom, as Sophie chatted about B-Bear and Pink. He closed the door behind us, and I sat Sophie on the bed, then crouched before her. How were we going to do this?

My gaze darted to Isaac, who appeared to be pained. He was hugging his midsection as if expecting a punch to the gut. I wished I could ease his mind somehow...

"Blocks?" she asked, pulling me from where my head had wandered.

"Yes, you can get back to your blocks in a minute. I wanted to tell you something important. Can you look at me?" Her pretty eyes darted from her skirt to my face. I smiled, and she smiled back. My heart thudded strongly in my breast. How was it possible to fall so deeply in love with another person so damn quickly? "We wanted to tell you that I'm your daddy."

She blinked, long lashes fluttering up and down. "Okay. Blocks?"

I threw a look up at Isaac, who shrugged. Then I returned my attention to Sophie. "Right, yes, we'll get back to the blocks. I just… we just wanted to let you know that I'm your daddy too. Do you understand?"

"I know. Daddy and Papa. Blocks?"

Okay then. Well, she was taking this incredibly well. Unsure of just how much the child really grasped, I nodded my head.

"So, you can call me Papa if you want. And your daddy will still be your daddy." That dug at me a bit, which was purely selfish, and I knew it. I'd have to work on that. What mattered most was what made life easier for Sophie.

"Good then. Daddy and Papa. Are you ready to go talk to the pretty lady?" Isaac asked.

"I has a skirt with ladybugs."

"Yes, you do." I stood, picked her up, kissed her cheek, and motioned for Isaac to lead the way. Katie grinned at us.

"Diaper emergency," Isaac said as he sat on the sofa. I

lowered my bulk down beside him, and Sophie sat between us on the floor, her lip between her teeth as she scribbled away at her coloring book.

After a brief hello and explanation from Katie, she set her phone on the coffee table and gave us an award-winning smile. She really was a beautiful woman. Pity I was too damn emotionally wrecked to truly appreciate her charms.

"Sophie, how are you feeling?" Katie opened with, easing us and the readers into things.

"Happy. I has two daddies now." She poked at me with a yellow crayon and then waved her crayon at Isaac. My mouth fell open. I threw a look at Isaac, who was just as stunned as I was. "And no bad sick blood."

Her innocent words hit me like a cannonball to the gut.

Two daddies.

Yes, she did have two daddies. And why not! Sure, Isaac was her uncle, but certainly we could explain that to her when she was older and able to grasp it. What was wrong with us both being "Daddy" and "Papa" for a few years? Nothing. Nothing at all. If she liked having a daddy and a papa, then who was I to grumble about it? Sweet Jesus why was I so damn dense!

"That's wonderful!" Katie beamed at the child. Sophie nodded then went back to coloring. Katie's hazel gaze lifted from my daughter to me. "You both must be so relieved and thrilled to have had such a wonderful outcome. Isaac, can you tell us a little about the tragic loss of your sister, Sophie's mother."

Isaac gathered himself, then softly began retelling a tale that I was sure the whole world knew by now.

Thankfully, his animosity to me didn't leech into the telling. He was pained, that was obvious, but as he began talking about Sophie and their time together, I could see the agony of his sister's loss leaving his eyes. He truly adored Sophie. Obviously as much, if not more, than I did. What had I been thinking wanting to hoard Sophie all to myself? Christ. I was such a fucking idiot. No wonder he'd reacted so violently. All he wanted was to be with his niece, and I'd shoved him aside in my quest to assuage my guilt over being such a drunken man whore. The longer he spoke, the more I felt some sort of life returning to me. This was what I wanted.

Not the interview of course, but Isaac and Sophie. Together. In my life. Two daddies and one precious little girl. My feelings for Isaac were more than desire, that much was obvious. I wanted them both in my life. And not just as an uncle or caretaker, but as the man I loved. *Why* did it take a boulder dropping out of the sky to get something through my thick skull! Somehow, I had to correct this before I lost him. God *above* why had I been so greedy! Vic would say it was the addict in me, and he would be right no doubt. Quite a few addicts could cop to being selfish. Not all, but many. Seems I was one of the self-centered ones. Just add that to a long list of faults that I'd need to work on in group.

Glancing from Isaac to Sophie as the interview went on, I mumbled things here and there, sticking Isaac with the bulk of the conversation, which was making him a little tense.

"Would you both like some coffee?" Isaac blurted out after a lengthy explanation of how he had tracked the boozehound—my word not theirs—down after Sophie's diagnosis had grown dire.

"Yes, please. Decaf with one creamer," Katie said while tapping at her phone. Bob nodded and asked for a black coffee. "Joachim, if you'd like to give me a hand?"

I followed Isaac into the tiny kitchen area. He turned to me, his blue eyes snapping with irritation.

"I know this is hard, but could you please try to add more than a grunt or a nod to the conversation?"

Staring down at him, my heart skipped along rapidly in my breast. I longed to kiss him and hold him.

"I will talk more. I'm sorry."

"This isn't the time to flake out on me—"

"I love you."

Chapter Seventeen

Isaac

THE GREEN POD OF DECAF COFFEE FELL FROM MY HAND.

"The fuck?" I saw the interviewer and photographer look over at us and lowered my voice. "What?"

Joachim picked up the pod and gave it back to me, grasping my hand.

"I want you *and* Sophie. Both of you. Together. This isn't a new thing. I just had it all locked up in my head, and I was giving too much space to everything else and not enough space to—"

"No." I turned back to the coffee.

"No?" he asked after a pause.

I snorted a laugh. "I don't know what you're doing, but this isn't a game. Help me take the coffees in, and by all that's holy, answer some damn questions."

"Isaac, listen to me—"

"No," I muttered and forced my way past him, back to the interviewer who stared up at me with wide eyes. How much had she heard? What was she going to write? I didn't want to be here right now. "Are we nearly done?" I asked her, and she took a moment to check her notes. She glanced up at me with a calculating stare—she was a shark in chum-filled waters looking for the kill.

"What's next for the three of you?" she asked, and I knew for sure that wasn't on the list because I'd explicitly said I didn't want to talk about the future in this interview other than a few generic responses about how lucky I felt for Sophie to have a second chance. This time though, she'd qualified the question to include the three of us, and now she waited for the answer. I didn't know what to say.

I was in shock.

"So, we're going to work hard on being a family," Joachim announced, and I couldn't move. He'd been so useless all interview and now he wanted to join in with such a bold statement? "The miracle of connecting to my daughter has changed my life, and I love our little family."

"And we're done," I leaped to my feet, "Sophie needs a nap."

Everyone glanced at Sophie, who was leaning against the sofa and yawning. No one could argue with the statement. In a flurry of movement, Katie and Bob began to gather their things. Joachim didn't move from his spot on the sofa. Sophie had climbed up into his arms and was dozing against her Papa J's chest. After a few polite goodbyes, I showed them to the door, but it didn't escape my notice that Bob, who still had his camera hanging around his neck, took some footage on his way out. What's the bet that the picture of Joachim cradling Sophie would be the photo that went with the headline.

Reformed hockey player, his daughter, and their miracle connection.

I held out my arms to take her from him, but he stubbornly held on.

"I was being selfish," he began in a low voice. "I never meant to hurt you."

I didn't want to talk. I wanted to hide away and think.

"You don't love me," I murmured.

"You must believe me when I say that I care for you. I can see what it is I want so clearly. It's you. And Sophie. And that little house across from Wigwam Pond. I want all of that." He shifted a little to make Sophie more comfortable, and she mumbled as she buried her face in his shirt.

All the affection and love that had been growing inside me began to push to the surface, past the anger and the distrust, but I couldn't see how this was going to end.

"We can be her two daddies."

"Not if you win," I said miserably. "If a judge thinks you're the better person for her, then what do I have? I can't fight that when I'm just her uncle."

He frowned and then sat up straight. "You're not *just* her anything, Isaac. You've cared for her this long, done everything for her, and you'll never be *just* her uncle. You're her father in every way possible, and I didn't see how important that was, not just as a label, but in every way. I was so focused on what I needed, or thought was right, that I didn't think about what Sophie might want. She needs you in her life."

"Thank you for seeing that," I said because I needed to be honest. Right?

He closed his eyes, so much emotion in his expression, and care and love in the way he cradled Sophie. "I didn't mean to fall in love with you, but it happened, and isn't that the best thing? It was accidental love." He looked so proud of that assessment. Accidental love? He was probably right about love being accidental, after all I'd met Joachim, and I inadvertently opened my heart to him as I watched Sophie get better, then I unintentionally fell in love without even realizing what was happening.

"I promise, me saying that isn't part of fighting for the right to be her legal daddy."

"How do you love me?" I asked. As Sophie's uncle? As a convenience? Or was it real?

He pressed a kiss to Sophie's head and stroked her back, pausing a moment as if he needed time to think. That wasn't a good sign, and I knew I was right.

"I love your beautiful eyes," he said finally. "I love the way you sing in the shower, the way you eat crackers in bed, the fact that you try to smile through pain just so that Sophie isn't sad. I love the way you kiss, the way you talk to me, the times you held my hand, the moments we shared when Sophie cried or smiled or called me Papa J."

I slumped to the sofa opposite him. What did he want me to say to all that? The need that I thought I'd pushed down was forcing its way past all my objections, and right now all I wanted to do was touch him. Kiss him.

"You want to know what else?" he asked with determination. "I love the thought of the future we could have together, the birthday parties, play dates, the dinners we'd make together, the moments watching a movie with Sophie, taking her to her first day of school together, teaching her to skate, seeing her thrive. Do you think you can love that the same way? Can you love me back, so we have a two-daddy life with Sophie?"

The fear of losing everything was an emotion I'd clung onto for so long—since the moment Ashley died, through the diagnosis, and now custody—that I didn't know how to not be scared. To let those seedlings of love see sunshine and grow was the scariest thing I'd ever considered.

"You recall that I asked my lawyer to file for official custody, right?" I asked, and he nodded as if that was perfectly fine. Was it fine? Was it okay to fight for her? Did I want to do everything on my own when I'd built so many dreams based on him being in our lives—my life? What in god's name am I doing? *Dealing with potential loss, being scared—terrified—avoiding pain.* Why didn't he yell at me and accuse me of stealing Sophie from him? How could he be so focused?

"If you want to go ahead and do that, maybe I won't fight for full custody. Maybe we share. But what I want is different to that. She has two daddies," he said as if that was the simplest thing on earth. "So, how about we go to the court, and we ask them to legally sign off that she has both of us as her fathers. If you can't love me, if you don't want us to be together, then we can have a proper shared custody because she needs both of us."

"Really?"

"You don't believe me?" he winced. "Am I saying it all wrong?"

I'm so scared.

I can't deal with any more loss.

Was it just the idea of us as a family that made it feel

as if I was falling in love? What is love? The only kind of love I know is connected to loss. I loved my parents, they died. Then Ashley died. Then Sophie got ill. I don't know how much more I can handle. I drew up my knees and wrapped my arms around them, pushed right back into the corner of the sofa. I wanted to cry and wail and let the desperation out of me until it was all gone. He watched me for the longest time in silence, and I tried my hardest not to crack, but my face was wet with tears. He carried Sophie into the bedroom. I heard him whispering to her, not the words themselves, but the gentle reassuring murmurs that would settle her.

Then he was back, and instead of sitting way over on the other sofa, he perched on the edge of the coffee table in front of me and rested his elbows on his knees, his eyes glassy with emotion.

"Will you marry me?" he asked.

I blinked at him. What?

He sighed. "Too much too soon? I know it is, but I want to do everything I can to make sure you know that this would be us together... the three of us. I can't move to Florida on this contract, but I don't have to sign another contract. We could live where you're happy, where Sophie will thrive. Or we could stay here in Boston. If I can prove I'm the skater they need, then I could stay with the Rebels, or hell, I could be traded. Or I could retire. But through all of it, it would be you, Sophie, and me together. What do you think?"

"Marry you?" That was all I could concentrate on; the rest was a mess of possibilities.

"My lawyer says that if we get married and then

petition together, we'd have equal rights. If that makes you feel more secure—"

"You want to marry me to make me feel secure?"

"No. Yes, no." He scrubbed his face and then sighed heavily. "I know it's a mess, but I love you. I want a future for us all where I get to wake up next to you in the morning and you come to the games, or not, and we take Sophie to school and play dates and go shopping for pink stuff or blue or yellow or whatever gender-neutral..." He stopped and took a moment to breathe he was talking so fast. "I love you, and I can't imagine life without you." He spoke those last words so quietly and with such emotion that my heart melted. "Can you forgive me for messing this up?"

He'd just proposed, told me he loved me, said all the right things. Had I waited too long? He moved to sit next to me then held out a hand. To take it I would have to uncurl myself, let go of my legs, get my hand free where I could hold his. I'd leave myself vulnerable, having to face all the fears and questions that were mixed up in my head... I didn't know if I could do that.

He didn't move his hand, just remained patiently still. Maybe I could have what he promised. Most importantly, he wanted to share loving Sophie, together. Not everything has to go wrong. Opening my heart again doesn't necessarily mean I'd have it shattered. Look at Sophie and how brave she'd been and how she saw only rainbows on a rainy day. Slowly I unlinked my fingers and gently took his hand. We stayed still for the longest time, and then he tugged me and guided me until I straddled his lap with my face buried in his neck. He wrapped me close, and I stayed still.

"I love you," he murmured, and it made me smile. All I needed to do was accept that I needed to live for today, trust that he wanted the best for Sophie, and we could make a brand-new family. Did I want that? Was that why I wanted to kiss him right now? Was that why I wanted to wake up Sophie and tell her that I loved her Papa J? I had to do this. I had to be honest with myself.

So, I sank deeper into his hug, and the words were easy to say.

"I think that I love you too."

I just don't know what happens next.

Chapter Eighteen

Joachim

"I LOVE YOU."

We'd both said it. Somehow, we'd both pushed aside the pettiness, insecurity, and pain to find what really mattered. Love. Love for our daughter and for each other. And I *did* love the man. There are those who'd say it was too quick. That love was impossible to experience in just a few months. That a couple needed to have years behind their relationship like Xander and Mason. Perhaps those doubters would be proven right. All I had was the present. I had no way to predict the future, and the past had been lived. As they say in meetings, we don't regret the past or want to shut the door on it. We have to learn from our past mistakes, see them, accept them, and atone for them. We also have to live for the day and for our futures. That meant staying sober and being honest.

"We should talk," he said

"Yes please." I sat down on the sofa and was quite

pleased to have him join me. He was uncomfortable, that was obvious. I was too, if I were being truthful. "Let's start with clarity and truth."

His blue eyes widened, then softened. "Truth. Yeah. We could use some of that." He blew out a lone breath. "I'm still scared of losing her." I opened my mouth to reply, and he pressed a finger to my lips. "No, you don't need to say it again. It's me. My fears. I just wanted you to know that I might have moments where I slip back into that fear. I'll try not to of course, but it won't be easy. I may mess up."

I rose just a bit and rummaged around in my front pocket. When my fingers skimmed what I was looking for, I pulled it out then motioned for him to hold out his hand. When he did, I dropped the little gold sobriety chip with the big 2 on the front into his palm. His gaze flew from the chip to me.

"We all mess up. We all falter and fall. We all have moments of doubt. Just know that when you feel yourself slipping you can come to me and tell me. You don't even have to say 'I'm really anxious about us' out loud. You can use a code instead if you wish, or if we're out in public." He gaped at me. "Say something like, 'Damn that gorilla' and I'll know you have a monkey riding your back."

"Damn that gorilla?" he asked. "What do you tell me when you feel weak and want to drink?"

"That I'm going to call Vic."

"Sure yes, of course you'd call your sponsor. I just thought…"

I cupped his chin. "I'd love to turn to you, but it's not a good idea for a loved one to be your sponsor. They say sex and romance can complicate the sponsorship role. Recovering addicts are incredibly vulnerable when we start a new relationship. And if we were to break up and you were my sponsor... well, it could lead to me falling off the wagon as I would have no one to talk to. I'm sorry."

"No, no, I understand. I'm glad you have Vic and AA to help you."

"Me too. I'm also really glad I have you and Sophie in my life." Cradling his chin, I leaned in for a kiss. It was meant to be just a peck, but as soon as his lips touched mine the spark lit the tinder. His mouth moved under mine, his tongue skimming the seam of my mouth. When I touched my tongue to his, he moaned and opened for me. The kiss morphed into a long, tender exploration of each other that somehow ended with him crawling over my lap. I grunted when his ass settled on my thigh. My glass was lifted from my hand and placed on the coffee table. The chip rested on the glass side table, shining bright yellow in the muted lights of the hotel room. When his gaze locked with mine again, I could see the desire flaring to life. I rested my hands on his hips, easing him up and forward.

"If I knew giving you a cheap token would get me kisses like that, I would have started giving them to you long ago," I teased, pressing my face into his throat to suckle on his neck. He gyrated against me.

"It's not cheap to me. It's a symbol. Trust and honesty." His fingers raked through my hair as he squeezed his knees tightly to the sides of my thighs. "I wish I'd not been such a flaming asshole. I wish—"

I covered his mouth with mine. He gasped then fell

into the kiss, sweeping his tongue over mine, his grip on my hair bordering on painful.

"We were both idiots. Let's focus on what we have now."

"A token and some kisses?" He rubbed my scalp, pulling a purr from me.

"Yes, and a new tomorrow."

"Two daddies," he whispered, gripping my head firmly and taking command of things. I sighed into the tasting, my hands sliding around to cup his ass. "I want you, but the stuff is in the bedroom," he panted as he rocked up. His prick rubbed against mine. I shivered with want, then nipped at his puffy lower lip.

"There are other ways," I panted, cradling his backside, lifting him upward just a bit. "Take out my cock and then yours."

"Yes, perfect… yes," he huffed as he fumbled with zippers and belts. The moment his dick nestled against mine, I nearly lost it. He held us tight, his grip firm, and began thrusting gently. Hands on his ass I brushed small kisses along his jaw and neck, saying whatever came into my head, words of love and admiration. Soft tender things that lovers whispered as they loved. His thumb slid over my cockhead, gathering precum, smearing it over the head of his prick then down the sides. He kissed my cheek, right where there was a small scar. My body was covered with scars. A testament to a life spent blocking shots and tossing the gloves.

"You're perfect," I whispered, wiggling him up just an inch more. I needed to feel his pulse throbbing against my lips when he came, which would be soon judging by his raspy breathing. "Beautiful, loving."

His fingers knotted in my hair as he pulsed and gasped. I buried my face in his neck as he rode out his release. The warmth of his spunk coating my dick nudged me closer to the edge. The sound of my name on his lips as he fluttered back down to earth pushed me over. I nipped at his neck, groaning as my body shuddered and quaked.

"So good." I heard him coo as he worked me gently, easing me down with slower and slower strokes. He nuzzled at my cheek, his nose warm, until I rolled my head. He stole a kiss, then another, and then another, our bodies cooling, our breathing steadying. "What is it about you?"

"My good looks?"

"Mm, you *are* ridiculously handsome."

"Ludicrously so," I replied, his breath fanning my face.

"Absurdly so," he countered. A small snort of amusement broke out of me. "Will you spend the night? In my bed? We won't be able to do anything but—"

I kissed him with all I had and then a dollop more. "I would love to spend the night. Are you okay with her seeing her two daddies in the same bed?"

"Mm, yes. Very much so. She should get used to it. I hope we'll be waking up next to each other from here on out."

I hoped for that as well. More than anything.

"As you enter the ancient elven ruins you pause, hands on the hilts of your weapons, to drink in the beauty of this hidden temple." Austin glanced over the top of his folding board, his eyes sparkling with anticipation, his official DUNGEON MASTER hat sitting proudly on his head. A gift from his boyfriend for his birthday last week.

"Are there any monsters in the area?" I asked.

Our young star studied me for a moment. "Give me a perception check."

I had no clue what that meant, but Robbie got me on the right path. I chuckled at the groans from my fellow adventurers when I rolled a one.

"Get some new dice would you!" Mason huffed just before a troll leaped out of the shadows and onto his back. Quite the fracas broke out as our band was surrounded, then pounded on by several vicious trolls. We all managed to survive, barely.

"Thank you for saving me the last time we played," I said to the table after the great troll battle wrapped up, and it was decided we'd better head home to our partners. Xander had to get home as Mason had a cold. Robbie was here with Austin. But I did have someone to get home to. Two someones. "Before we all clear out, I'd like to make a small announcement."

"You're the most piss-poor paladin in all the land?" Moral tossed out. I wasn't sure if he was joking or not until he gave me a sassy wink.

"Yes, aside from that. Isaac has officially moved in with me."

"Is that the big announcement?" Xavier asked as he placed each die into a small velveteen bag, his brown gaze rather bored. I glanced around the table. No one seemed to be impressed or even interested.

"Well… yes," I said.

"Hey, they made it official and that's big. Congrats, Loafer," Xander stated in true captain style.

Ugh. Damn Moral and his asinine nicknames. As if what my sponsor called me wasn't bad enough? Moral hadn't been happy with his previous attempt and so had called me Loafer during a presser about the new children's cancer ward the team was donating to the hospital that had handled Sophie's case with such professionalism and care. Now I was stuck with it. Rather like poor Austin would be Peachy until his dying day.

"Did you all not think we would?" I enquired of my teammates.

"No, we were just wondering what was taking you so long," Austin replied, which got a laugh or two from the guys.

"Seriously, we've known forever that you two were going to end up together," Xavier said and got nods from all the others at the table. "But congrats."

"Yeah congrats," they all chimed in as they gathered their paraphernalia.

"It's been over a month since he moved in. Back in," I said just because it felt like our announcement of living together should warrant more excitement.

"Yep, and we're super happy for you guys. Sophie has two daddies," Robbie said with a smile as he helped Austin gather up their stuff.

"Yeah, it's awesome! We have to split. Renco is in one of his weird moods, and I hate leaving him alone when he's all sullen and spooky." Austin gave me a wan smile, grabbed his board and books and papers then split with Robbie.

"Is he sick?" Xavier asked. "Renco? Is he sick?" he enquired again when we all looked at him with confusion.

"I don't think so. He's just a goalie. You know how they are," Moral tossed out, then pushed to his feet, stretching his arms over his head, then rolling his neck. Bones popped and crackled. We all winced. "Remember that time we all showed up at his place drunk and he nearly took off your head with that paddle of his, Cap?"

Xander chuckled and nodded. Talk then leeched away from my big announcement to olden days before I was a member of the Rebels.

"We're going to make a party invitation and invite all of you. For dinner. To cement our status as a real couple," I loudly announced.

"I'll be there," Moral declared while shrugging into a thick brown wooly coat that made him look just like Fozzie Bear. "There *will* be food, right?"

"He said dinner," Xavier commented, then placed his bag of dice into a little leather case that he'd made just for his adventuring goodies. "Dinner usually includes food, doofus."

Moral flipped us all off as we chuckled at the interplay. We called out goodbyes to each other then stepped out into the brutal cold November winds. Winter had blown in a few days ago. I was not a fan. I'd wanted to take Sophie to Wigwam Pond tomorrow as we had three whole days off for Thanksgiving, but the cold might end that thought. We had a road trip after the holiday that would take me all over Canada, and I'd be gone for two weeks. I loathed the idea of leaving my man and my little girl for that long. I'd even balked about coming here to play tonight, but Isaac had insisted I attend. And with Renco backing out, I was needed it seemed. Damn trolls.

"Hey, Loafer, you know we're all tickled pink about you and your guy, right?" Moral asked as he caught up with me on the sidewalk. "We're just busting your balls, you know."

"Yes, I know." And I did. It had taken me some time, but I was now feeling as if Boston, and this team, would be my forever future. I could see myself retiring here as Isaac's art career exploded. We'd raise Sophie in this welcoming city that had embraced me so openly where I had my support system here. My meetings, my sponsors, my friends, and of course my role-playing group. But we could split the time down to Florida where Isaac and Sophie belonged. Whatever we did, we would do it together. "And thank you for busting my balls. I truly feel like a Rebel."

Moral barked out a laugh, then slapped my back so soundly I stumbled forward a step. The man was a moose.

"There you go! We only bust the balls of those we love." He grabbed my face and planted a loud, wet smooch on my cheek before ambling off, the wind whipping at his long red beard. Wiping my face while sniggering madly, I made my way to my car, climbed in, and called home.

"Hey, are you guys done already?" Isaac asked right off.

"Yeah, Austin was worried about Renco. He's in one of

his dark, hiding moods it seems. So, I'm heading home. Do we need anything from the store for tomorrow's feast?"

"I forgot the cranberry sauce, if you'd like to grab a couple of cans?"

"Yes, of course. Anything else?" My nose was cold. Damn this winter weather. Victor only laughed when I had started complaining about it a few weeks ago. Sweaters and hats, coats, and mittens. Yuck. Still, it did have its charms. Cuddling in bed on a chilly, gray day with a sexy man was perhaps one good thing about the cold. That and the pink cheeks it gave my beautiful daughter. I could not wait to see her reaction to snow. Okay, so perhaps the winter had a *few* good things about it. But just a few.

"The only thing I want is you home and in this bed. Sophie just went down."

"Should I buy some lube?"

"Yes, and some cherries."

"Cherries? For Thanksgiving dinner tomorrow or for bedtime tonight?"

"Bedtime."

"I'll be home in twenty minutes."

"I'll be in bed, waiting, naked."

Lord help me. "I'll be home in ten minutes. With lube, cranberry sauce, and cherries."

The look I got from the cashier when I checked out with all those items at the Market Basket was priceless.

Epilogue

Isaac

16 years later

"Adam, leave your sister alone!"

I'm glad it was Joachim dealing with the kids and not me.

I was lucky enough to be the one driving our family to visit Sophie for Christmas at college, which by unspoken agreement left Joachim to handle our other two children, Adam and Meghan.

It'd been a long car journey from Boston to Charlotte, not in miles or hours, but in the level of excitement from Adam, who was at the height of being an annoying ten-year-old, and Meghan, who was now thirteen and far too grown up for her own good.

"I wasn't doing anything," Adam said as if butter

wouldn't melt, but I caught sight of him in the mirror, and he was still poking at Meghan's leg, which was going to end up in an epic showdown if we didn't stop things now. I caught Joachim rolling his eyes at me with a wry smile, but I reached over and caught his hand and held it tight for a few moments. We were in this together and that meant parenting Sophie, Meghan, and Adam as a team. Sometimes Joachim slipped into Coach mode and his warnings became orders, whereas sometimes I went into artist-world, truly a place, and I let things slide, but between us, we'd done a pretty good job of being dads.

"Stop poking me," Meghan snapped.

"Adam," Joachim warned with a loud sigh.

"Freak," she added.

"Meghan, please ignore him, and, Adam, for all that's holy leave your sister alone."

"Five minutes to go," I alerted everyone, and for a few moments, there was silence. We were all excited to see Sophie, that was the problem, and tensions were high and exacerbated by back-to-back traffic into Charlotte. All too soon we pulled up in the parking behind the dorms, banners for Christmas events hung from trees, kids scurrying around as if they all had a purpose.

And then I saw Sophie waiting under a tree, holding hands with a young guy who joined in with the wave she threw us.

"Who the hell is he?" Joachim muttered.

"Her boyfriend," I said with a smile. Joachim too fatherly protection to the extreme.

"Did we bring a shotgun?" Joachim grumped.

"No, but we can go back and get one if you want one," I replied, and then we exchanged a look—the one that spoke of late nights and worry and love and happiness when there was no sign of cancer, no illnesses of any kind other than the usual ones, and the fear that one day she wouldn't be ours to look after anymore. He opened the door, corralling Adam and Meghan until they ran ahead and were swooped into a three-way hug with Sophie. Joachim held back. I held back.

She was beautiful—as beautiful as her mom—and every time I looked at Sophie, I felt the tug of grief that I doubted would ever leave me. Ashley would have been so proud of Sophie, graduating school with honors and getting a place at her first-choice college to study art and dance. Over the top of her sibling's heads, she grinned at us, and Joachim took my hand so we could saunter over together as if neither of us wanted to run like the wind to get our hug.

The five of us held each other and laughed. Sophie told us she missed us, and we said it back. I wanted to cry because our kids were everything to us. When the hubbub died and the hugs were less, Sophie tugged the young man forward, an earnest looking boy in a white shirt, tie, and smart pants. He'd really gone all out to make an impression.

"This is Cole," she announced.

"I'm so pleased to meet you, sirs," Cole said addressing us with a respectful use of the word sir, shaking our hands firmly, then gripping Sophie's hand. We did our best dad looks, the ones that threatened bodily harm if he hurt our little girl. In fact, Joachim crossed his arms across his chest.

"You'll never guess what, Papa?" Sophie said with a wide grin. "Cole plays hockey!"

I hid my smirk when Joachim stiffened, cursed, then stepped right into Cole's space.

"Hell, if our daughter is dating a hockey player," he growled, but Cole swallowed and met him head on.

"Papa, don't." She rolled her eyes, just like her father, then turned to me who normally calmed things down. "Dad, do something."

"Sir, I love Sophie," Cole interrupted.

"You've only known each other, what? Three months," Joachim muttered.

"Babe—"

"Hockey players are… *players*." He shook a hand at me, and I noticed that Sophie guided Cole, Adam, and Meghan away. I cradled his face, looking into his beautiful hazel eyes. He'd been sixteen years sober now, the best dad, the very best husband he could be, and I loved him more each day, if that was even possible.

"It will be okay," I said.

"How do you know?" he grumbled, but there was a hint of a smile there as well.

"I just do."

He rested his hands on my hips, and I stretched up for a kiss.

"I love you, Isaac. But if he makes her cry…"

I chuckled and gave him one more kiss. "Then I'll hold your coat, and give you an alibi."

"In it together?" he asked, and now he was smiling.

"Always."

THE END

What's next for the Rebels

Snowed

A second chance at love is all Renco wants for Christmas, but a dark menace from his past wants him dead, and suddenly love is second to staying alive.

Kyle 'Renco' Lourenco has carved out a comfortable life and career for himself in Boston. With the holidays quickly approaching, he's heading home for the first time in several years. Home to his loving parents and the small Canadian town where he grew up. Home to shinny games, his mother's poutine, and his father's lame dad jokes. Home to Christian, his best friend and the first man to steal his heart. Renco's hopeful that this visit to Eagle Ridge will ease the nightmares that he's suffered from his entire life. Nightmares that painted the holidays with a malevolence he could never escape.

As a winter storm blows in, Renco is stranded at the airport miles from home as a dark and sinister force from his past creeps ever closer. His only hope is getting to

Christian's cabin before the evil that has haunted him for years finally catches up to him.

Best friends since they were three, Christian grew up next door to Renco in a remote mountain town with one stoplight and a forty-mile round trip to the nearest school. When Renco left town for a shot at a professional hockey career, he took Christian's heart with him. Even though he knew Renco was always destined for bigger things, it hadn't stopped Christian from falling for him as soon as he knew what love was.

With Christmas in three days and storm Tabitha heading their way, Christian shuts the doors to the family store and heads to his cabin to be on standby as an official volunteer for Search and Rescue. His life hasn't changed much from one year to the next but finding out that Renco is coming home, even if it's for a few days, leaves him restless and angsty. He doesn't regret staying in Eagle Ridge, but a near miss on a simple rescue leads him to reevaluate everything, and when Renco ends up at his door, he knows that guarding his heart might not be the best solution after all.

Hockey Series' from RJ Scott & V.L. Locey

Harrisburg Railers

Owatonna U Hockey

Arizona Raptors

Boston Rebels

LA Storm

Chesterford Coyotes - Young Adult

Free Reads

Please note - in all of these free stories, there will be some spoilers for the main series books.

Railers Short Stories

LA Storm

The Colts - AHL Short Stories

Standalone

Harrisburg Railers

When hockey wunderkind Tennant Rowe meets his new coach, he knows he's in trouble. Jared Madsen is nine years older than Tennant, impossibly attractive, and — worst of all — his brother's off-limits best friend. Is their chemistry worth the risk?

Changing Lines (Railers 1)

Can Tennant show Jared that age is just a number, and that love is all that matters?

The Rowe Brothers are famous hockey hotshots, but as the youngest of the trio, Tennant has always had to play against his brothers' reputations. To get out of their shadows, and against their advice, he accepts a trade to the Harrisburg Railers, where he runs into Jared Madsen. Mads is an old family friend and his brother's one-time teammate. Mads is Tennant's new coach. And Mads is the sexiest thing he's ever laid eyes on.

Jared Madsen's hockey career was cut short by a fault in his heart, but coaching keeps him close to the game. When Ten is traded to the team, his carefully organized world is thrown into chaos. Nine years his junior and his best friend's brother, he knows Ten is strictly off-limits, but as soon as he sees Ten's moves, on and off the ice, he knows that his heart could get him into trouble again.

Changing Lines

Harrisburg Railers (Hockey Romance)

1. Changing Lines
2. First Season
3. Deep Edge
4. Poke Check
5. Last Defense
6. Goal Line
7. Neutral Zone
8. Hat Trick
9. Save The Date
10. Baby Makes Three
11. Rivals
12. Perfect Gifts
13. Family First

Railers Volume 1 | Railers Volume 2 | Railers Volume 3 | Railers Volume 4

Meet the men of Owatonna University's hockey team

Ryker (Owatonna U, 1)

Ryker

Ryker is hockey royalty, Jacob is a poor country boy. Can two vastly different people find common ground and become the men they want to be?

Ryker comes from a long line of championship-winning hockey players. Playing college hockey to develop his game is his only focus, and nothing will stand in the way of him working to become the best player. He has no room for relationships, people who point out his flaws, or anyone who calls him on his dreams. He certainly has no place for love, and meeting Jacob is nothing but a useful distraction on the side. After all trying to get his Owatonna Eagles teammate into bed is less work and more play. When tragedy rocks his family, his charmed life crumbles, and the only person he can turn to is the same one who claims to hate him.

Jacob Benson has only known hard work and stifling conservative values his whole life. Born and raised in the small rural community of Eden Crossing, Minnesota, he's the only son of a hard-working but struggling dairy farming family. Jacob is using his skills in hockey to finance his way to an agricultural science degree. These four years at Owatonna U. will probably be the only time he has to enjoy life, gain acceptance about his sexuality, and live openly before his inevitable return to the farm. Running into a pretty rich boy like Ryker Madsen is putting a damper on his enjoyment of life away from home. Ryker's flip, conceited, carefree attitude grates on Jacob's every nerve. So why, if Ryker is everything he dislikes, does he want nothing more than to explore the sinful dreams that his annoying teammate stars in every night?

Ryker

Owatonna U Hockey (Hockey Romance)

Coast to Coast (Arizona Raptors 1)

Coast To Coast

**When opposites attract, this bottom-of-the-league team will
never be the same again.**

A stipulation in his father's will forces Mark back into the arms of
a family that disowned him and leaves him one-third owner of a
hockey team facing financial ruin. He doesn't even watch hockey,
let alone like it, and wants nothing more than to head back to
New York. Then there's the new coach, a stubborn, opinionated,
irritating man with superiority issues and questionable music

taste. Butting heads with Rowen becomes the new normal, but it comes with passionate debate and an all-consuming lust.

Challenged to rebuild one of the worst teams in the league into a future cup contender, Rowen can't pass up the opportunity. Never in his twenty years of hockey has he ever seen a team managed so badly or coached players overflowing with resentment and bigotry. Yet there's something about this team and this city that compels him to roll up his sleeves and start dismantling. If only Mark, one of three siblings who now own the Raptors, wasn't so damned rock-headed yet so damned appealing his job might be easier. It doesn't look like either is willing to give in, but one night in a dark, desert hotel changes everything.

Coast To Coast

Arizona Raptors (Hockey Romance)

1. Coast To Coast
2. Across the Pond
3. Shadow and Light
4. Sugar and Ice
5. School and Rock

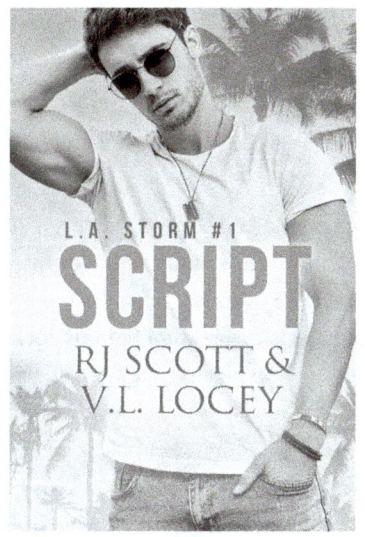

Script (LA Storm, 1)

Script

Hollywood A-lister Finn might be Canadian, but he needs Cameron to show him how to hockey.

Actor Finn Kerrigan is at a crossroads. After growing up a soap star, then starring in a hugely successful trilogy of action movies, he's finally given the chance to read a heartfelt and passionate script that could change his life forever. The role would be enough for people to see him as a serious actor, and maybe even win him an award or two (and no, a golden raspberry award for his action movies doesn't count). Once established as a serious actor he's sure he can come out of the closet and finally live his truth. When he lies to get the part of a hockey player on a struggling team, he suddenly has nowhere to hide. He might be Canadian, but the last time he skated he was ten, and no, he doesn't have hockey in his blood. With only a month until filming starts, he about to be exposed, but partnered with a player who's supposed to be giving him tips, he doesn't realize how many of his secrets will come to light. Falling in lust, one heated kiss at a time, is inevitable, but giving Cameron up at the end of the shoot could break his heart.

Cameron Chavkin is the face of the LA Storm. And the body, and the hair, and the smile. He's at the prime of his career, men and women want to be with him, and he's skating better than he ever has before. His house sits next to a famous rock star's mansion, his garage is filled with expensive cars, and he's even been asked to mentor a once-famous actor in a new hockey movie. Life is pretty sweet. Until the bad boy of hockey meets Finn, a man on the edge with more secrets than Cameron has endorsements. Knowing better than to get involved, Cameron is swept up despite himself, and when it's time to say goodbye to the Storm's most eligible bachelor is finding it hard to follow the script.

Script

LA Storm

1. Script
2. Second
3. Shield
4. Spiral

Off The Ice (Chesterford Coyotes, 1)

Off The Ice

A coming-of-age love story with high school, hockey rivalry, friendship, family, and coming out.

Soren's life changes in an instant when he and his younger brother are adopted by hockey royalty. Making sense of his new life is hard enough, but when he's enrolled in a private school it means facing a whole new set of problems. Navigating friendship, family, and hockey is one thing, but being attracted to the boy who vexes him is a whole new thing.

Felix has a reputation to protect. He's the kid who seems to have everything but looks can be deceiving. Spinning lies about his perfect life, he's created a fantasy world that even he has started to believe. Only, it's not long before everything crumbles, all of his pretty lies are revealed, and only his closest rival sees through his pain and stands by him.

Fighting is easy, friendship is hard, but love is everything.

Off The Ice

Chesterford Coyotes

1. Off The Ice
2. On Thin Ice
3. *Dance on Ice*

Also By RJ Scott

For a full list of ebooks and links please scan the code above or visit rjscott.co.uk/rjbooks

Meet RJ Scott

RJ discovered romance in books at a very young age and realized that if there wasn't romance on the page, she could create it in her head. With over one hundred and fifty books published, she is a full time author of gay romance.

She lives and works out of her home in the beautiful English countryside, spends her spare time reading, watching films, and enjoying time with her family.

The last time she had a week's break from writing she didn't like it one little bit and has yet to meet a box of chocolates she couldn't defeat.

www.rjscott.co.uk | rj@rjscott.co.uk

NEWSLETTER - rjscott.co.uk/rjnews

facebook.com/author.rjscott

x.com/Rjscott_author

instagram.com/rjscott_author

amazon.com/author/rj-scott

bookbub.com/authors/rj-scott

goodreads.com/rjscott

pinterest.com/rjscottauthor

Also By VL Locey

For a full list of ebooks and links please scan the code above or
visit vllocey.com/stories-from-vl-locey

Meet V.L. Locey

V.L. Locey loves worn jeans, yoga, belly laughs, walking, reading and writing lusty tales, Greek mythology, the New York Rangers, comic books, and coffee.

(Not necessarily in that order.)

She shares her life with her husband, her daughter, one dog, two cats, a flock of assorted domestic fowl, and two Jersey steers.

When not writing spicy romances, she enjoys spending her day with her menagerie in the rolling hills of Pennsylvania with a cup of fresh java in hand.

vllocey.com
vicki@vllocey.com

Newsletter - vllocey.com/newsletter

facebook.com/V.L.Locey

x.com/vllocey

instagram.com/vl_locey

bookbub.com/authors/v-l-locey

goodreads.com/vllocey

pinterest.com/vllocey